Two Crazy

Bust a Move
Book Two in the Val Fremden Midlife Mystery Series
Margaret Lashley

What Readers are Saying about Two Crazy:

"A crazy, laugh-a-minute mystery. Twists, turns and mishaps keep you from putting the book down! A must-read series!

"If you want a fun, suspenseful, and downright crazy book to read this summer this is definitely your pick."

"I loved this book as I have come to love the crazy dysfunctional characters who make you laugh out loud."

"I can completely relate to (Val) and her crazy life. What makes these books so good is that they are really close to true life... And I love that right off the bat I'm laughing!"

"Laugh-out-loud funny and entertaining from start to finish."

"One of the best series I have read in YEARS!!!"

"You have to love the main character and her band of misfits, intriguing and hilarious all at once."

"I absolutely love how this writer writes. I need more Val in my life!"

More Hilarious Val Fremden Midlife Mysteries

by Margaret Lashley

Absolute Zero
Glad One
Two Crazy
Three Dumb
What Four
Five Oh
Six Tricks
Seven Daze
Figure Eight
Cloud Nine

"Why does life always have to give me the finger?"

Val Fremden

Prologue

(**S**poiler Alert! If you haven't read Glad One yet, you may not want to read this. If you've read Glad One, then, well, go for it!)

I'm Val Fremden, aka Thelma Gladys Goldrich, aka Valiant Stranger. A double life wasn't good enough for me. So I decided to make it a triple.

Last year, a bulldog-faced woman named Thelma Goldrich called me a tramp and knocked me out cold at Caddy's beach bar, right before the memorial service for an old beach bum named Tony. That punch in the nose turned out to be the best thing that ever happened to me.

Long story short, Thelma's right hook to my poor schnoz set in motion a chain of bizarre events that changed my life forever. I discovered that Justas and Lucille Jolly were not my biological parents. My real parents were a couple of crazy, beer-guzzling, beach-bum hoarders named Tony and Glad Goldrich. They both died within days of each other and named me—*their biological, long-lost daughter*—as sole heir to their tiny, junk-filled house on the Intracoastal Waterway in St. Petersburg, Florida. Oh yeah. They also left me enough cash to keep me in chocolate bars for a long while to come.

Good thing, too. At the time I was like, *seconds* away from being homeless.

I also found out that my *real* birthday was December 22nd. But I decided to keep celebrating it on April Fools' Day, like I had for the last forty-eight years. Given the weird scenario surrounding this particular

5

aspect of my life—correction—given the weird scenario surrounding *my whole life in general*, it just seemed...well...totally *on the nose*.

I'd figured out this twisted story with the help of a cop named Tom Foreman and three washed-up derelicts named Winky, Jorge and Goober. I'd rewarded the three burn-outs with $5,000 each. The cop, well, let's just say he got something else out of me.

Chapter One

The tread-worn, whitewall tires squealed on the hot asphalt. I shifted into park and climbed out of Shabby Maggie, my 1963 Ford Falcon Sprint convertible. Like me, Maggie was creamy-white and a bit girlie on the outside, but underneath her hood beat a V8 engine that could kick butt with the big boys.

I'd been cruising along Gulf Boulevard, a block from the beach, when a thought latched onto me like a starving mosquito. I pulled a one-eighty in the middle of the road and made a beeline for the drugstore at the corner of 107th in St. Pete Beach.

It was my birthday, and I was going to celebrate it in style with a king-sized Mounds candy bar. I knew for a lot of folks, that wouldn't have sounded like much of a present. But for me it was. I *never* kept chocolate at my place. It was the only thing I couldn't be trusted with.

I high-tailed it inside the store and grabbed a candy bar from a rack by the register. A minute later, I strolled outside with both chunks of delicious, gooey heaven crammed into my mouth like Lucille Ball at that chocolate factory. Distracted by the commingling of chewy coconut and rich, dark chocolate, I didn't notice someone was in Maggie's passenger seat until my butt was already wedged halfway in on the driver's side.

When I caught sight of her, just inches from me, I totally freaked.

I jerked back and let out a high-pitched scream that could only be heard by dogs and dolphins. Before my brain could put two-and-two together, I swung my purse at her and busted her square in the face.

As my pocketbook hit pay-dirt, I had what I called an *idioment;* an idiotic moment of doomed recognition—like seeing the car keys hanging in the ignition just as you slam the locked door shut. There was no turning back. I'd have to live with the consequences. I sucked in a surprised breath and nearly choked to death on chewed-up coconut.

"Aaarrrgh! Oh crap!"

I cringed. My eyes doubled as she flew backwards off the seat and tumbled onto the floorboard. Dressed as she was, no one in the whole world would've recognized her except for me. It was Glad—still wearing that plastic Mr. Peanut piggybank she'd been shaking around in the very last time I'd seen her, less than an hour before her botched burial at sea last year. That day, someone had taken Glad from my car in this very same parking lot. Today, they'd returned her. And on my birthday, no less. I wasn't sure if that qualified as ironic or not, but the timing was definitely weird.

Whoever Glad's kidnapper had been, he'd left a hand-written note on the seat. I picked it up. The torn scrap of yellow paper read, "Sorry. Mr. P."

I glanced around the parking lot. None of the tourists milling around the place looked like perverts or body snatchers. (Well, maybe one.) I picked Glad up, hugged her to my chest, and set her back on the passenger seat beside me.

I turned the ignition and smiled.

It may sound crazy, but over the rumbling of Maggie's twin glass-pack muffler, I'd swear I heard Glad say:

"Screw you, Kiddo."

I turned and gave her a wink.

"Nice to see you again, too, Mom."

Chapter Two

Owning a home again was turning out to be a blessing and a curse. It was nice to be able to fix things up the way I wanted. But dealing with the renovations and repairmen had me cursing under my breath—*in German. Scheisse!*

I'd moved into Glad and Tony's old 1950's ranch house yesterday. Now, not even twenty-four hours later, the blasted air conditioning had died.

When I'd been renting, I'd just picked up the phone and said, "Come fix this." Those days were over. *I* was the responsible party now. And I didn't have a clue who to call. The only person I could think of was my next-door neighbor. I'd seen her a few times while I'd been working on the place. She'd waved and seemed friendly.

What the heck. I'll introduce myself and see if she knows someone who could fix it....

I rang her doorbell. I didn't get a referral. I got an *eyeful*. The door opened wide, and standing before me was a woman wearing nothing but a pink thong bikini bottom, sparkly stilettos and enough gold necklaces to sink a rowboat. I think Mr. T would have made her an official member of *The A Team* if it weren't for one thing.

She must have been around seventy years old.

If a geriatric donkey and one of those wrinkly little Shar Pei dogs had a baby, it might have grown up to have a mug just like this woman's. Her long, horsey face was the color and texture of spray-tanned crepe paper. When she cracked her mouth open and smiled, I half expected her to whinny—or bray. In fact, it was kind of surreal when she *spoke* instead.

It was like being trapped inside that old TV show with *Mr. Ed's* trashy girlfriend.

"Howdy, neighbor!"

The tall, thin woman spoke down at me from her vantage point about a foot above my five-foot-four frame. She thrust out a hand, sending her cadre of necklaces and both boobs swaying. I tried to keep my eyes off the pendulum action.

"Hi. I'm Val Fremden. Just moved in next door."

"Seen you moving in. Nice to meet you. I'm Laverne Cowens."

"Uh, I can see you're busy, Laverne. I don't want to take up your time. Just wondering if you knew a good air-conditioning repair company?"

"On the fritz, huh?"

"Yes."

"Well, I know a thing or two about air conditioners. Let me see if I can help you out."

Before I could object, Laverne turned around and disappeared down the hallway, her shriveled, spray-tanned butt cheeks wobbling around a corner. A moment later she reappeared wearing a sparkly gold beach cover-up. I sighed with relief.

"Show me that air handler thingy."

"Uh, that's okay. I just need a ref—"

"Nonsense! What are neighbors for?"

Laverne closed the front door behind her and shooed me toward my place with a liver-spotted hand spiked with pointy, red fingernails. She followed me across the lawn, high-stepping through the grass with her long, orange legs like a stork through a salad. I led her through my front door and into my small, open-plan living room and kitchen, then down a hall to the closet where the old air handler unit was installed.

"Nice place you got here."

Laverne's donkey head shifted left and right, causing her gold hoop earrings to jangle underneath her smooth, strawberry-blonde hair cut in a soft, layered bob. Her bug-eyes rolled the full range of their sockets.

"I like the green paint in the kitchen."

"Thanks. Not much to see at the moment. I'm still putting the place back together."

"Glad and Tony *did* let things get a little rangy around here, that's for sure."

"You knew my parents?"

"A little. But they mostly kept to themselves. Once in a while, Glad would talk to me over the fence. But not too often. In fact, I didn't even know they had a daughter until *you* showed up."

"That's understandable."

I thought about explaining how I hadn't known it myself until a few months ago, but I was in a hurry and wanted to keep on topic. I opened the closet door and hit the light switch. Nothing happened.

"Huh. The closet light isn't working," I muttered absently.

"Hmmm...but your *kitchen* light *is* working," Laverne remarked. "That's strange. Are you sure you paid the *whole* light bill, honey?"

I snickered. Laverne's face showed genuine concern.

"Uh. Yeah, I think so."

Laverne cocked her head like a puzzled dog and scrunched her horsey brow. I figured I'd better do something to distract her before she blew a gasket in that worn-out little brain of hers.

"Uh...I'll go get a flashlight," I fumbled.

I padded to the kitchen and grabbed a big black flashlight from the cupboard below the sink. I shone it into the closet. Laverne peeked in and shook her head.

"Aha! Just what I thought! That's a Trane!"

She pointed a shiny red fingernail at the brand name etched into a silver plaque on the air conditioner's dull, dusty, olive-colored housing. "See? It says here, T-R-A-N-E."

"So, what's the problem? Is that a bad brand?"

"No. Duh!"

Laverne shot me a pathetic look. She shook her head softly and pointed at the logo again.

"See here, Val? It was made for a *train*, not a house."

My mouth fell open. I stared at Laverne like a dead trout in a seafood display case. She smiled back sweetly, like a kindly old school-teacher. I almost expected her to pat me on the head. She punched me softly on the arm instead.

"First house, huh, sugar? You'll get the hang of it."

"Wow. Well...uh...thanks, Laverne. Sorry to have bothered you."

"No bother at all, honey! Happy to have you around! You just call me any old time you need me."

"Thanks. I sure will," I said as I steered her skinny butt to the door. I meant it, too. Because at that moment in time, I couldn't conceive of a single scenario where I would ever need her help again.

THE BUSTED AIR CONDITIONER was just the latest item on a mile-long list of repairs my parents' dilapidated little house had need-ed to make it inhabitable again. Just sorting through and hauling away decades of accumulated junk had taken months. Living with Friedrich's hoarding issues in Germany had prepared me somewhat for the mess, but he'd been an amateur compared to Glad and Tony. Together, they'd accumulated literally *tons* of garbage. It was everywhere, strewn from the rafters in the attic to the far corners of the backyard. Among their neurotic stash of loot was every magazine printed since 1985, around twenty-million almost-used up toilet paper rolls, fifty million assorted twist ties, bread bags and yogurt cups, a ball of used tinfoil big enough to choke a blue whale, and swollen cans of fruit cocktail and succotash purchased during the Carter administration.

But the biggest shocker came when I'd unearthed a mummified black-and-white cat in the back bedroom. Squashed nearly flat under an avalanche of *Cat Fancier* magazines, there was no telling if it had been my parents' cat or some unfortunate stray. Or worse yet, one of the neighbors' precious pets. I'd stuffed the dried-up carcass in a *Hello Kitty* bag I found under the bed, threw it in the dumpster and never said a word to anyone.

After clearing away the mountains of crap, I'd gotten started on repairs; new roof, plumbing, electric, water heater, etc. It was German déjà vu all over again as I'd watched my bank account drop like the gas tank indicator on a Hummer stretch limousine. Finally, toward the last week of February, I'd seen the light at the end of the repair tunnel and felt it was safe to give my landlord notice. My goal had been to move into my new place before my birthday. But I knew full well that things didn't always go as planned. After all, I was the middle-aged poster child for how life could suddenly take a U-turn and dive off a cliff. Armed with that knowledge, I'd covered my bases and paid the rent through the end of April.

As it turned out, that decision had been more money down the drain. But I wasn't complaining. After scrubbing and painting every room in the house, I'd managed to get the house livable before the end of March. Yesterday, March 31, I'd piled my belongings into the backseat of Maggie and moved from my ratty, closet-sized apartment downtown to my palatial, thousand-square-foot house on the Intracoastal Waterway. I'd owned next to nothing, so the move had only taken one trip.

I smiled at the idea of never having to go back to that place. Yesterday, I'd tossed my last handful of clothes onto the pile in the backseat and cranked Maggie's engine to life. My landlord was gone on vacation, so I'd dropped the apartment keys in the mailbox. There'd been no one to wave goodbye to, so as I'd driven away I'd extended my middle finger to the ugly-ass brown couch I'd 'inherited' from the last tenant. I'd left its sagging old carcass in the alley, along with my memories of the eighteen months I'd spent there as a lost, friendless, derelict-in-training.

Fun times.

Chapter Three

With my meager belongings all tucked away in my new place, I was celebrating my good fortune. Tonight I was throwing a birthday-cum-housewarming party. The air conditioner had died, but it was just the first day of April. It wasn't full-on summer yet in St. Pete. We still had a few good weeks left before the sweltering heat and humidity came and squatted its sweaty, sunburned butt on us and robbed us of our will to live.

My party guests for the evening included the regular gang, Goober, Winky, Jorge, my parents' estate attorney J.D. Fellows, and, of course, my boyfriend Tom. Earlier today, when I'd realized I was the only woman attending, I'd thought about inviting Laverne from next door. But given her low IQ and clothing-optional lifestyle, I'd decided she'd been too sketchy.

Now that it was almost party time, I was revisiting the thought. *Laverne too sketchy for this crowd?* I laughed under my breath. *A spoon-sucking peanut head, a crazy, freckle-faced redneck, a Latin lager lout, a barnacle-sized barrister, and a cop with whom I'm committing crimes of passion...and I'm worried about* Laverne *being too sketchy?*

I checked the fridge. It mirrored my guest list. The usual suspects. A cheese tray. Carrots and celery. Ranch dip. Chicken wings. A case of Fosters. Tonic and lime. I made a mental note to work on my lineup of both food *and* friends.

A cool blast hit my face when I opened the freezer. I clunked three ice cubes into a highball glass. Next to the ice-cube trays, a half-gallon, emerald-green jug of Tanqueray stood frosty and alone except for the company of two frozen, chicken potpies. The pies were my "going-out insurance." I *hated* pot pies. Tom despised them even more than I did. Whenever he came over and asked what was for dinner, I'd pull out the pot pies. He'd take one look and say, "Let's eat out." I'd put the disgusting things back in the freezer, and they and I would live to fight another day. Like Rita's booze bottles back in Germany, my pot pies were "only for looking."

I poured a shot of gin into my glass of ice and rummaged around the fridge for the lime and tonic. It was getting close to six. The party was in half an hour. Just enough time to get a quick shower and a TNT buzz....

THE DOORBELL RANG AT 6:30 on the dot. I pinned back my damp hair and thanked my stars that I was almost dressed. I pulled a light sweater on over my tank top and jeans and padded barefoot to the front door.

"Hey there, Val Pal!" bellowed Winky as I opened the door.

To my surprise, the short, ginger-haired redneck wore pants that reached all the way to his bare feet. Stretched over his freckled beer belly was a clean Hawaiian shirt—still sporting every single one of its buttons. And, be still my heart, a brown tweed sport jacket! Compared to Winky's normal raggedy attire, this qualified as a tuxedo. His effort made me smile.

"You 'member Winnie?" Winky hooked a thumb to his left and a short, pudgy girl with black hair and red glasses stepped into view.

"Oh! Sure. From Water Loo's. Nice to see you again, Winnie."

"You, too, Val." Her brow furrowed. "You don't mind I came along, do you?"

"Oh. No! Not at all! You're more than welcome. I could use a girl to talk to. Come on in!"

"Thanks!"

Winnie showed her teeth, making her puffy cheeks rise like hot biscuits. Her eyes squeezed into curving slits like an Asian Buddha. Combined with her short-cropped, jet-black bob and bangs, she made the perfect Japanese anime character. I stepped aside to let the pair enter, then hooked Winky by the arm as he tried to pass by.

"Are you two *together?*"

Winky grinned like a poorly carved Jack-o'-lantern.

"Yep. Shackin' up for nearly a month now. Good thing, too. I got tired of campin' in the woods all by my lonesome."

"I thought you and Goober—"

"Nope," he said, cutting me off. "He took the money you give him and got hisself a place downtown. Near *your* old 'partment, I think."

"Oh. Well...congratulations. On Winnie, I mean. She's really cute."

Winky puffed himself up.

"Hey now, Val. Keep yore facts straight. Winnie's got the car and the job. *I'm* the one's got the looks."

My head wagged involuntarily from side to side. I wasn't sure if Winky was joking or really thought himself a prize. With men, you never could tell.

"Right."

Winky grinned and slapped me on the back. "Dang straight! Got any beer?"

"In the fridge there's—"

Winky took off like a future train wreck, my words trailing behind him like piss in the wind. Winnie followed after him at a slightly slower pace. I turned to face the door again and saw tall, lean Goober standing there, wagging his bushy eyebrows at me. He lifted his Rays baseball cap from his bald pate and set it back again. *The act of a true, Florida gentleman.*

Broody, mysterious and perpetually inebriated Jorge stood beside him. Even though Jorge and I were the same height, he rarely looked me in the eyes. He preferred to stare at my shoes. Tonight, he'd have to settle for my bare feet. Both he and Goober sported stubble beards tonight, but they'd showered and put on clean clothes. I could tell because they smelled like the April Fresh Downy packets they sold at the laundromat.

"Hey Val," Goober said. "Where's the beer?"

"Wherever Winky is."

"Cheers." Goober raised one eyebrow and made a straight shot for the kitchen. Jorge was hot on his heels like a droopy hound dog.

I started to close the door when I heard a noise.

"Haruuummm."

I looked down and saw the diminutive J.D. Fellows, Esq., standing at the door. Dressed in khaki slacks, a short-sleeved yellow shirt and a light-blue sweater vest, he looked alarmingly like a lawn jockey.

"Oh! Hello Mr. Fellows!" I nearly shouted. I tried to hide my amusement by faking surprise. "Come in!"

"Thank you, Ms. Fremden."

The attorney straightened his four-foot tall frame and took a tentative step inside. He surveyed the living room like a man used to keeping an eye out for danger.

"I always wondered what your parents' abode looked like on the inside...minus all the...*extraneous paraphernalia*, that is."

"You mean hoarder crap? Yes, it looks a lot bigger without the tons of garbola."

"Yes. It certainly—"

"Hiya, hottie."

The familiar voice, deep and sexy, grabbed my attention and curled my toes. I turned to see Tom, my law-enforcement lover. He was leaning against the doorframe, demonstrating his unique brand of laidback, Southern gorgeous. His sea-green eyes twinkled, as if they held a secret just for me. The brawny, blond cop always took my breath away, but tonight he looked like a cowgirl's dream come true in his denim jeans and blue, button-down shirt rolled up to his elbows.

"Brought you a little housewarming gift," he teased. "An old friend."

"Really? Who?" I looked around, but didn't see anyone.

"Well, it's more like a 'what' than a 'who.'"

Tom pointed to the street where his vehicle was parked. Hanging halfway out of the back of his Toyota 4Runner was that butt-ugly couch I'd left on the curb to fend for itself or die. Apparently it had fended for itself.

"What the...?"

"Happy forty-ninth birthday," Tom said with a smirk.

"Gee, thanks, Tom. It's just what I always wanted."

Chapter Four

I woke the morning after my birthday party with a cop in my bed and a dead body in the kitchen. Okay, it was just a roach carcass. But I swear it was big enough to draw a chalk line around. It was legs-up in the middle of the floor. I'd fumbled, bleary-eyed, toward the cappuccino machine in nothing but Tom's t-shirt, and had managed, of course, to step right on it. The disgusting crunch of its carapace underfoot made me scream like a little girl.

"Aaahhhh!"

As a native of the Sunshine State, I'd grown up learning to deal with the worst that Florida's flora and fauna had to throw at me. Poison ivy. Cabbage-palm spikes. Daddy long-leg spiders. Fire ants. Kamikaze tree frogs. Ghoulish house geckos. Deadly rattlesnakes and cottonmouths. Even the occasional gator on the road or in a swimming pool. I'd managed to make my peace with all of them—except one.

Let a roach get anywhere near me—especially a flying one—and my bravado disappeared faster than Oreos at a Weight Watcher's convention. When I'd stepped on that nasty bug, I'd let out a scream that could be heard on the International Space Station. If that marked me as a sissy, so be it. But there was something abhorrently primeval about a creature that could live for months without its own head.

"What's going on in there!?"

Tom dashed into the room. He was naked except for his state-issued revolver. The sight of his tan, muscular body almost made me forget about my predicament. *Almost.*

"A roach," I grimaced. I held up my foot like it needed stitches.

Tom grinned at me and shook his head.

"There appears to be no permanent damage. What happened to my fearless partner? Valiant Stranger?"

"Hey. Roaches are my kryptonite, okay?"

"Duly noted. I thought you put out some traps. Roach Motels, right?"

I took a paper towel off the roll and ran it under the tap. I bit my lip in disgust and wiped my foot.

"Yeah, I did. I guess there was no room left at the inn."

Tom sniggered. "Don't those things come with 'No Vacancy' signs?"

"Very funny, Mr. Morning Sunshine. Can we please change the subject now?"

"Okay."

A dirty grin crept across his face. Tom sidled up to me and put his hands on my hips.

"Have *you* got a vacancy that *I* can fill?"

I knocked his hands off of me.

"Geez, Tom. I think that may go down in history as the most disgusting foreplay line *ever.*"

Tom scooped me up into his arms. His naughty grin deepened his dimples and crinkled the corners of his hypnotic, green eyes.

"Okay, how about this? I've got a gun, lady. Better do what I say."

Both my hormones and my imagination went haywire.

"Now *that's* something I can work with."

AFTER ALL THE CRAPSHOOT relationships I'd been in, I kind of hit the jackpot with Tom. He was good looking *and* he was good with his hands and other assorted body parts. When it came to pleasing me, he'd proven to be a quick study. In fact, this morning he'd just aced another oral exam before he'd disappeared into the kitchen.

Yes. High marks all around.

I smiled up at Tom from the bed as he padded back into the room carrying two toasty, yummy cups of cappuccino sprinkled with cinnamon, just the way I'd learned to love them in Italy. I sat up and stuffed a pillow behind my head. Tom handed me a cup and crawled in beside me. My rickety little full-sized bed creaked under his weight. I suddenly wondered if it creaked when we made love. *Funny, I never had the presence of mind to notice....*

"Off in Lady La La Land already this morning?" Tom teased.

"Are you calling me an airhead? Fair warning. I'm armed with scalding coffee."

"Aww shucks," Tom said playfully. "All sweetheart this morning. And you haven't even had your first sip yet."

I smirked and raised the cup halfway to my lips and stopped.

"If you didn't make such good cappuccinos, I'd be mad as a hornet at you, Tom Foreman. Whatever possessed you to bring that hideous sofa over here? That roach probably came along for the ride."

"Dang it! And that freeloader died before he paid me my cab fare."

I giggled and elbowed Tom in the ribs, nearly spilling my coffee in the process.

"It's not funny," I said, trying not to laugh. "It's disgusting!"

Tom winked devilishly. "Come on now, sugar doodle. Don't be like that. I only had to shoo three cats and a possum off-a that there couch. I didn't see no roaches."

"Enough with the hick routine, okay?"

"Yes ma'am." He set his cup on the nightstand and snuggled next to me. He kissed me on the shoulder and whispered in my ear. "I *like* that couch, Val." His warm breath tickled my neck. "We've had some great times on it."

"I didn't know you were the *sentimental* type," I said, but I knew full well my sarcasm was no match for his persistent sexiness.

"*You're* obviously not."

"Not when it comes to flea-infested furniture."

Tom gently took my cappuccino from my hand. His tan, muscular arm reached across me and set the cup on my nightstand. He kissed me on the lips, then began to nuzzle my neck. I closed my eyes....

All of a sudden, a familiar whirring noise caught my attention. I sat up in bed.

"What's that sound, Tom? Hey, wait a second...."

"What now?" Tom sat up on an elbow.

"I think the air conditioner compressor just kicked on."

"I thought it was broken."

"So did I."

I jumped out of bed and made my way to the hall closet. I opened the door. Sitting atop the old air handler was a crumpled note scrawled in child-like handwriting. It read: "Gaul-dang great party, Val. Thanks."

"Winky!" I yelled.

"Winky?" Tom called from the bedroom. "Is he crashed out drunk in there?"

"No!"

Winky had disappeared for a while during the party last night. I'd assumed he'd just gotten hammered and passed out somewhere. But he hadn't been up to no good. He'd been up to *good*. A smile slid sideways onto my face. *That freckle-faced little redneck rascal.* I closed the closet door and padded back to the bedroom. Tom wasn't there. I lingered in the doorway, collecting my thoughts. A moment later, Tom came up behind me...in more ways than one. Either that, or he was still toting that gun....

TWICE IN ONE MORNING was my limit, so I showered, dressed, and left Tom in bed reading the Sunday paper. A big smile had settled on my face about Tom and me, and I wanted to keep it there. I jumped in Shabby Maggie and rumbled off to Water Loo's, the chosen hangout of my deadbeat friends, Winky, Jorge and Goober.

The wonderland of ironic fodder dished out by Water Loo's never ceased to both amuse and appall me. The rat hole disguised as a restaurant was the kind of dingy, hole-in-the wall place that could never hope to rise to the esteemed status of, say, a run-down, truck-stop diner. Hobbling along on its last legs for years, Water Loo's was being run—*into the ground*—by Loo, a disgruntled ex-pat Brit and his potty-mouthed girlfriend Latrina. The fact that both of their names were not-so-subtle monikers for toilets propelled them, in my mind, to the reigning king and queen of the St. Pete irony scene.

The two burned-out restauranteurs appeared to have given up on the idea of quality and service so long ago that it was no longer even a distant, plaguing memory for either of them. Instead, their sole goal in keeping Water Loo's afloat was to make enough money to bet the afternoon trifecta at the Derby Lane greyhound track. This habit, along with their wanton inattentiveness to customers and cleanliness, offered me a daily-double dose of delicious irony whenever I overheard them yelling from the kitchen that their lives were "going to the dogs."

Which, actually, was pretty often. From what I could tell, their love of gambling was second only to their love of griping and complaining. Loo and Latrina could be counted on to burst into shouting matches at any given moment. Occasionally, it escalated to pushing and shoving, but more often than not, neither sticks nor stones broke anyone's bones, but the cuss words they hurled were foul enough to curdle the creamer.

As a result, Water Loo's clientele had dwindled to a mere trickle. Nowadays, it was frequented solely by hard-core locals. Mainly those with no other choice due to DUI-related lack of transportation or severe, blinding hangovers. On the rare occasion, their ranks would be boosted by the random lost or grossly misinformed tourist.

But Water Loo's did get *one* thing right. It lived up to its name. It was a total crap hole. The final splash down spot for the effluence of humanity as it passed on to its foul, inevitable end. That's why I was pretty sure that the gang would be there this morning. I cracked open the door and took a peek.

"Hey Val Pal!" Winky shouted.

He was the first to spot me from his vantage in the corner booth. Peanut-headed Goober turned around and gave me a silent salute, his long fingers grazing the top of his shiny, hairless pate.

"Look who's all bright bald and bushy lipped this morning," I chirped as I walked up.

"Yeah, and look who just got laid," Goober said, shooting me a sneer of mock annoyance. "I like you better when you're a sourpuss in the morning."

My face grew red as the guys snickered amongst themselves.

"Scoot over, butthead." I shoved Goober on the shoulder.

Goober muttered complaints under his breath and scooted his butt across the greasy vinyl. I slid in beside him and he stuck a spoon in his mouth. I blanched when I realized I'd grown fond of the tinny, hollow sound the utensil made as he clicked it against his teeth.

"Great party last night," Jorge slurred.

The Latino's blue-black hair, usually wavy, looked more like a tsunami this morning. His big, puppy-dog brown eyes rolled lazily in his skull, unable to focus. Despite his inebriated state, I could have kissed Jorge's drunken lips for changing the topic.

"Thanks Jorge. Did you enjoy yourself?"

"I don't remember," he managed to blurt, just before his head hit the table.

Mr. Dude whiskey had claimed its first victim of the day. I turned my attention to the two guys still clinging to consciousness. Actually, they both seemed pretty sober this morning, all things considered.

"Thanks for fixing my air conditioning, Winky. I didn't know you were handy."

"Oh, he's handy all right," joked Goober. He pointing his spoon at Winnie, who was busy doing nothing behind the coffee counter. "Ask her yourself."

"Good 'un, Goober!" Winky chortled.

The two slapped hands in a high-five. Winky turned toward me. His freckled face shifted from silly to serious in the blink of an eye.

"You know Val, I can fix purty-near anything with a pocketknife or a roll a duck tape."

"You mean duct tape," I corrected.

"That's what I just *said*," Winky huffed. His ruddy face tinged a shade pinker. "Get the cotton's balls outta yore ears."

"Yeah, Ace Face over here was an auto mechanic until things got all computerized," Goober explained. "Ain't that right, buddy?"

"Yep," Winky nodded solemnly, then grinned. "I don't know nothing about no *mother boards*. Less'n you count the one my momma used to beat me on the hind-end with."

I sniggered despite myself. "What did *you* do for a living, Goober?"

Goober took the dull silver spoon out of his mouth and laid it on the table. He twitched his lips, causing his bushy moustache to undulate like a furry, brown caterpillar.

"Drove a cab, mostly. Up in New York City. But then they found out I spoke English and had a good sense of direction. That was the end of that."

"Ha ha," I said dryly. "I heard you moved downtown. How do you like it?"

"I could get used to walls and indoor plumbing again." Goober smoothed an errant whisker with his thumb and forefinger

"So, where's your new place?"

"I prefer to remain anonymous of domicile, Val. Besides, you've already got a boyfriend. *Obviously.*"

The two men grinned at each other like hyenas at a fresh kill.

"What do you mean, *obviously*?"

They broke into a wave of raucous laughter. It echoed dully off the restaurant's greasy, brown-paneled walls.

"What's so funny?" I demanded.

My question set them off laughing again.

"Come on. Tell me!"

Goober raised a finger, tried to speak, then cracked up laughing. Winky finally managed to utter a few words between hillbilly hoots and guffaws.

"Val...your...gaul-dang...shirt's...on...inside...out!"

Chapter Five

I left Water Loo's in a huff. I was totally *peeved* at the men in my life. *Ha ha ha. The joke was always on me. Jerks!* And not *one* of them had brought me a birthday present! It wasn't like I'd expected something nice from the gang, but come on? Not even a chocolate bar? Tom hadn't given me a gift either. Not unless I was counting that couch. And believe me, I wasn't!

I mashed Maggie's gas pedal to the floorboard. She blew out a cloud of built-up carbon. I turned the radio on full blast. It drowned-out the obscenities I hurled at the sunburnt tourists shuffling along Gulf Boulevard. I was madder than my cousin Tammy when the new stylist at Beauty Belles botched her haircut right before her fifth wedding.

I desperately needed an unsuspecting target to unload my frustrations on. One that couldn't talk back. A thought hit me like a hammer between the eyes.

That crappy sofa. That disgusting thing was going to get the cleaning of its life!

I'd have chucked that piece of crap sofa yesterday if I hadn't needed it for the party. I'd ordered a new couch weeks ago. It was supposed to have arrived on my birthday. But while I was unpacking my stuff from Maggie's backseat, I'd gotten a call from Couches Today. The delivery had been delayed for another week.

Couches Today? What a joke! They ought to call that place "Couches Some Day." No, "Couches Maybe Some Day."

Geez! I was in such a bad mood I couldn't even make a decent joke!

I squealed up the driveway and slammed on the brakes. Tom's silver 4Runner was gone. *Good. There would be no witnesses. Bring it on, sofa.*

I marched into the house. My sandals skittered across the floor as I kicked them loose. My purse sailed across the room, grazed the armchair, belched its contents across the terrazzo floor, slammed against the wall and sunk to the floor like a punched-out drunk. I snatched the lumpy brown cushions off the couch, pushed the sliding glass backdoor open with my bare foot and flung each one into a heap on top of a plastic lounge chair. I grabbed my weapon of choice from the kitchen. Dust plumed like a mushroom cloud with every whack of broom-straw on corduroy.

I was almost done pulverizing the first cushion when I heard someone call my name.

"Hi Val!"

I glanced sideways from my frenzy like a disrupted serial killer. My horse-faced neighbor Laverne was in her backyard, waving at me. This time she was fully clothed...in a shiny gold lame robe and matching heels. At least I had *that gift* to be grateful for. I waved back half-heartedly.

"Wanna cup of coffee?" she yelled from the low picket fence dividing our properties.

"I'm kinda busy," I yelled back.

I raised the broom and whacked a poop-brown cushion for emphasis.

"You should always take time to stop and smell the roses."

Laverne walked over to the white fence reached out her hand.

"Here."

I let go of my stranglehold on the broom handle. Laverne held out a small bouquet of white, orange and pink roses. I dropped my broom and a little bit of my witchy mood and met her at the fence.

"Thanks, Laverne."

I took the roses from her hand. Inbred Southern guilt crawled up my throat and out of my mouth.

"Why don't you come over to *my* place for a cup of coffee?"

"Don't mind if I do!"

Laverne hiked her robe up to her hips, stepped over the fence with her spray-tan-orange stork legs and followed me inside. She ogled the kitchen with her big donkey eyes while I poured coffee into two huge novelty mugs. Hers read, "World's Best Something or Other." Mine read, "I Like Big Cups and I Cannot Lie."

"I see your faucet's leaking."

Laverne was sitting at the breakfast bar, staring at the kitchen sink.

"Yeah." I shrugged. "Another thing on my to-do list."

"Maybe I can help."

Before I could object, Laverne jumped up and busied herself jiggling the tap handle. The stainless-steel double sink had a pivoting faucet that swiveled to reach both basins. Laverne swung the spout from one sink to the other, then back again. I kept one eye on her as I searched the fridge for the cream. She was totally tongue-out focused on her task.

"You take sugar or cream, Laverne?"

"Huh?" Her eyes shot up at me for a millisecond. "Oh. Neither."

Her googly eyes returned to the faucet.

"Okay," I said. "Here's your—"

"Ah ha!" Laverne called out. "I got it!"

"Got what?"

"It's not leaking anymore, see?"

I looked at the faucet. She was right. No *drip, drip, drip.*

I handed her a mug. "What did you do?"

She set the mug on the counter. "Watch."

Laverne moved the spout about an inch to the right. The water started dripping again.

"So?" I asked.

"See? If you move the thingy to five p.m. on the clock dial, it quits leaking."

She adjusted the tap again, her tongue sticking out of the corner of her mouth to aid her efforts.

"See? No more leaking."

"Wow. Tthanks, Laverne," I said dryly. "Another problem solved. But tell me again. The position that stopped the leak. Was it five *a.m.* or five *p.m.*?"

"Five *p.m.*, definitely."

Laverne sat back and cocked her head proudly.

"Okay, I'll remember that," I said. *I couldn't forget it if I* tried.

Laverne's naïve, cheerful ignorance made me question how she'd managed to survive to such a ripe, old age.

To be totally honest, it also made me envious.

I was completely devoid of the gene required for Laverne's brand of happy-go-lucky bounciness. I wondered what life must be like for people like her—those lucky individuals who were never bothered by the need to ponder the reason for anything. I couldn't seem to escape questioning *everything*—from the purpose of my existence to why a grown-ass man wouldn't buy me a decent birthday gift.

"You okay in there, sugar?"

My attention shot back to the room. Laverne was staring at me like a mother donkey.

"Oh, sure. I was just wondering, Laverne. How'd you learn to be so...*handy*?"

"Oh. I was a Vegas showgirl!"

As if that explained everything.

THE HOUSE I INHERITED wasn't, in itself, much to look at. It was just a single-story, concrete-block box with terrazzo floors, an open living room, dining room, kitchen area, two bedrooms and one small bathroom. But the location was a whole different story. After Laverne left, I went outside to gather up the battered remains of the sofa cushions. As I reached for the last one, a boat horn sounded. I looked up and was reminded that my backyard had a breathtaking panorama of the nearly always sunny and sparkling Intracoastal Waterway.

When I'd first gotten the house, the backyard had been a garbage dump. Literally. But after all the junked appliances, broken windows, garbage bags and dead cars had been hauled away, a whole new perspective had come into view. Even now, with nothing but weeds and bald patches of sand for landscaping, the seascape was spectacular. The only thing blocking my wide-open water vista was Glad's old Minnie Winnie RV. It remained, still parked, flat-tired, in its little patch of weeds. I just couldn't bear to part with it.

From where I stood, the wide, turquoise waterway sparkled like diamonds in the sunlight. Small, wooden docks jutted out along the saltwater inlet like teeth on a sawfish's boney nose. Along both sides, modest homes in pastel hues made the waterway feel more like a cozy, liquid lane, with boats replacing cars parked along its edges. The overall effect was, ironically, both expansive *and* cozy. I stopped dead in my tracks and drank it in for a moment. *Lavern was right. It does pay to stop and smell the roses.*

When I hauled the sofa cushions back into the house, an odor punched me in the nose. It *wasn't* roses. It emanated from the area around the couch, and smelled like a dead frog's fart. I dropped the cushions on the floor and peered under the sofa. *Nothing.* I climbed onto the cushion-less frame and felt around in the crevices where the bottom of the couch met the back. I came up with three pennies, a plastic spoon and a laundry token. I tried the space by the right armrest. My fingertips detected something wedged in the crack. I curled my fingers around it and pulled it out.

It was about the size and shape of a hotdog. Whatever it was, it was wrapped in a white handkerchief. I unfolded the cloth and stared, open mouthed, at a gold ring engraved with the initials WH. It was still encircling a bloated, grey, human finger.

Chapter Six

It was a little late in life, but I'd just discovered another thing that made me scream like a little girl.

"Calm down, Val!" Tom said over the phone. "Put it in a jar with some ice."

"Are you out of your mind? I'm not touching that thing!"

Bitter bile surged up my throat. I wretched.

"We need to preserve the evidence," Tom said in his cop voice.

"Then I suggest *you* come over and do it!"

I clicked off the phone and ran toward the bathroom. I high-jumped past the area in the living room where I'd flung the finger away in horror. I locked the bathroom door and dry-heaved into the toilet. I stuffed a towel under the door, in case that horrible finger came back to life and tried to inch its way after me.

The logical part of my brain knew that the whole idea of a reani-mated finger was irrational. The scared-witless part didn't give a flying crap what my rational part knew. I needed to keep my feet off the floor and away from that finger! I squatted on top of the pink toilet-seat lid and remained perched there, like a frozen pigeon, until I heard the door creak open and a familiar voice call my name.

"Val? Where are you?"

"In here, Tom!" I called from behind the bathroom door. "I'm not coming out until you deal with...*it!*"

"Roger that."

Tom burst out laughing.

"It's *not* funny!"

"I'm not laughing at the *finger*, Val."

"Well, you better not be laughing at *me*, or you're going to get *another* kind of finger!"

Tom laughed again.

"I'm on it, Miss Marple."

The panicked horror that had gripped me for the last fifteen minutes like a popsicle in King Kong's fist suddenly thawed and sent me tumbling off the toilet. I grabbed the towel bar on my way down and snatched it off the wall. We both fell to the floor with a clattering thud. Tom was at the door in an instant. He tried the knob, but it was locked. I wasn't taking any chances with that finger.

"You okay in there?"

"Yes, I think so." I hauled myself up, still clutching the towel bar in my right hand. "Where's the finger?"

"Apprehended. In a pickle jar. You're safe."

I cracked open the bathroom door and looked up at Tom. His face was plastered with a boyish grin. I kept a firm grip on the towel bar and held it like a club behind the door, in case that hideous finger escaped from that jar.

"You better be telling the truth! No funny stuff!"

Tom's face returned to normal, which for him meant devilishly handsome.

"Scout's honor. I never joke about evidence."

"Then why did you call me Miss Marple?"

"First of all, *you're* not evidence, Val, so joking with you is fair game. Secondly, you fancy yourself a detective, Valiant Stranger, but you crumple at the least little thing. And third—"

"A finger isn't a *little* thing!" I shot back. "I mean, it's not a *big* thing...but...aargh! Anyway, I never said I wanted to be a detective. And I *didn't* crumple!"

Tom grinned. "Tell that to your towel bar."

"Very funny."

I dropped the metal bar. It clanged on the tile floor as I closed the bathroom door behind me.

Then I tiptoed down the hall behind Tom and glanced around the living room and kitchen. "Is it still in the house?"

Tom raised an eyebrow. "Do you really want to know?"

"No."

"Okay then. Now tell me how you found it."

TOM AND I SAT ON THE stools at the kitchen breakfast bar. I poured us each a glass of iced tea and explained how I pulled the finger out from a crevice in the sofa.

"With my bare hands!" I finished, whining in horror.

Tom studied my hands for a moment then eyed his glass of tea warily. "Better bleach your hands."

"I did already. Like, six times, if Ty D Bol counts."

Tom tried not to smile.

"That ought to do it. How do you think the finger got in the couch?"

"How should *I* know? You're the one who hauled the mangy thing back from the alley. Were there really three cats and a possum on it?"

Tom brushed a strand of brown, wavy hair from my forehead.

"No. Just a bum taking a nap."

"What!"

I screeched and punched Tom on the arm, nearly knocking him off the stool.

"Why didn't you tell me?"

"Hold on there! At the time, I didn't think anything of it." Tom regained his perch on the stool. "The guy couldn't have been lying on it for more than an hour or two. He seemed okay. I gave him a fiver to help me load the sofa into my 4Runner."

"Was he screaming when you left?"

"What?"

"You know. Something like, 'Hey mister, my finger's in that couch!'"

"Not that I noticed."

I gloated. "So *who's* the crummy detective *now?*"

TOM CALLED THE COPS. They came to the house and one of them asked me a bunch of questions. I answered them while Tom talked to the other cop and handed over the pickle jar with the finger in it. They hauled it and the couch away as evidence. I figured that would be the end of it.

Boy was I wrong.

Chapter Seven

Two days had passed since the couch had given me the finger. Then I'd gotten another one from Couches Today. When I'd called this morning to ask when to expect delivery on my new sofa, they'd basically instructed me not to hold my breath.

I would have been ticked off, but it was Tuesday. That meant Tom would be taking me out tonight. Even though we were in the habit of spending three or four nights a week together, the cop and I still kept our separate places. We also kept a standing Tuesday-night date we'd begun when we first started seeing each other last year. I called it Taco Tuesdays. That always made Tom smile.

It still stung a little that Tom hadn't bought me a real birthday present. But I was trying to rise above it. After all, I'd lived through so much worse. Considering all the lousy presents I'd received over the years from my ex-husbands, that ugly-ass couch didn't even make the top three. Those esteemed positions were held by a jar of jalapeño peppers (sole Christmas present), a cheap silver necklace with a plastic four-leaf clover (fourteenth anniversary) and a walnut press. (Really? I mean, *really*?) In my opinion, those beat the couch hands down in my "WTF were you thinking" rankings.

Still, it bugged me. If I was going to stay in a good mood for Taco Tuesday, I needed a pick-me-up. I knew just where to get it. On the way home, I stopped at a funky little boutique on Corey Avenue and bought a pink floral top to wear with my black jeans tonight. Tom liked me in pink, and turning Tom on was never money wasted. As I drove back to my place, my mind was filled with visions of Tom peeling off my new blouse. I nearly hit the mailbox pulling in the driveway....

I stripped and turned the tap on full-blast in the vintage flamingo-pink bathtub. All the repairmen who'd tromped through the house in the past six months had advised me to tear out the old 1950s bathroom, but I just couldn't bear the idea. I guess I felt nostalgic—not just about the architecture, but about the parents I never really knew.

Except for a casual "hello," I'd not once spoken to my father, Tony Goldrich. I'd seen him around Caddy's beach bar plenty of times. But back then, I hadn't known he was my biological father. He'd simply been the itinerant beach bum raking the sand and picking up garbage. I'd met Glad, my mom, on Sunset Beach next to Caddy's. We'd talked a lot. Often for hours. I'd gotten to know her pretty well in those six weeks before she died.

I squeezed a good measure of rose-scented bubble bath into the water and watched it foam into merengue-like peaks. I wondered if Glad had liked bubble baths as much as she had enjoyed a cold pint of Fosters. Or bright-red lipstick. The thought of Glad's beef-jerky hide soaking in the pink tub made me feel at home, somehow. My decision to keep the bathroom intact had really been about holding on to a piece of *them*—a piece of *my real family*. I smiled and lowered myself into the steamy froth.

Ten minutes later, I hauled myself, naked and pink, out of the tub. I reached absently for a towel and came back with a handful of air. I made a mental note: "Get a new towel rod." I grabbed the towel I'd laid across the toilet seat and wrapped it around me. I fiddled with my damp hair in the mirror and looked at the small photo of Glad I'd found when I was clearing out the house. I'd taped it to the vanity mirror. I stared at her image, then at my own reflection. I liked to think I looked a bit like my mom, but I wasn't sure.

The photo of Glad had been taken not long before she passed at the age of 65. In it, she was smiling that crooked, red-lipstick smear of a smile, sprawled out in the sun like a frog on vacation. Her long, Slim Jim arms and legs spilled over her pink lounge chair, stuck in the sugar-white sand at Sunset Beach.

I smiled. The photo had captured Glad perfectly, in her element, doing what she loved. She didn't have a care in the world as she hoisted that pint-sized can of Fosters between her boney, brown fingers. I kissed the tip of my finger and touched it to her face. Then I slipped into my bra and panties and got ready for my date with Tom.

I LOVED TACOS, AND Red Mesa Cantina in downtown St. Pete had some of the best. Tom and I parked on Beach Drive in the free, three-hour parking zone between Fifth and SixthAvenues. It was a bit of a haul to Red Mesa from there, but it was a nice walk. And it saved money. I wasn't destitute anymore, but those days had taught me not to needlessly throw away my cash. But even more than that, I found it hard to relax and enjoy the evening when I had to constantly think about feeding a parking meter.

Tom and I strolled hand-in-hand past the romantic, posh and pink Vinoy Hotel, then skirted the oak-shaded park offering glimpses of yachts bobbing on the calm, harbored waters of Tampa Bay. The sky was tinging pink, and a tiny chill crept in on the early evening air. I shivered. Tom untied his sweater from around his neck and draped it over my shoulders. He looked into my eyes like I was the only woman in the world.

"I really like you in pink," he whispered in my ear.

Goosebumps popped up on back of my neck.

"Really?"

"But I like you even more in nothing at all."

A wave of electric lust shot through me. *Man, it's hard to stay mad at a man who likes me naked. Maybe that's enough of a birthday present—him liking me in my birthday suit.*

We cut through the evening crowd in front of the Birchwood Hotel. The streetlamps kicked on. I spotted a street performer about twenty feet in front of us. I pointed at him.

"Look, Tom! How cool!"

The man had a deep, baritone voice. But his words sounded strangely hiccoughed and slurred. As we drew closer, I realized the man was singing the *Star Spangled Banner*. But it didn't sound quite like singing, exactly. Weirdly, the performer was bent over like a quarterback waiting for a hike. My teeth clamped together and started grinding. *What the?* The man was *belching* and *farting* the national anthem *for tip money!*

Tom burst out laughing. I punched Tom on the arm.

"Don't laugh! That's horrible! It's disrespectful!"

Tom put his arm around me and tried to hold me back, but I was hell-bent on giving the offensive jerk a piece of my mind. I marched up to him—*too* close to him as it turned out. The guy broke wind in my face!

A second after sniffing a face-full of fart, my purse found its mark on the man's backside with a dull thwack. He whirled around. Our eyes locked. My mind did a double-take. My mouth fell open like a wallet at a strip club.

It was Goober.

My anger evaporated in the roasting heat of social embarrassment. My neck, moments before chilled to goosebumps by Tom, turned scarlet-hot with shame. I tugged at Tom's arm, trying to escape. I wanted to take him—and any lingering chance of a nice evening—along with me. But it was too late.

"Hey, Val." Goober said. "Not a fan of Le Petomane, I take it."

"What?" I demanded, whirling around to face him.

"The famous French fartiste," Goober explained, as if he were talking about Picasso to a preschooler. He wore a ragged old top hat and a crumpled, red-striped bowtie, like a down-and-out Uncle Sam.

"You've got to be kidding me!"

"I most certainly am not. Le Petomane was considered royalty in his day. Highest paid performer at the Moulin Rouge. His real name was Joseph Pujol. I'm a distant relative, you know. Though I only recently discovered my latent genetic talents."

"There's...there's no such thing."

"Look it up," Goober challenged. He stuck his nose in the air. "Oh, the tortured life of a *flatulist*. So few appreciate our true talent."

"But you were belching, too!" I argued, as if that somehow disqualified him from such a high-brow profession.

"Yes. Poetic license. The prerogative of every fartiste."

I didn't want to stick around to see what else might come out of Goober.

"Let's go, Tom."

I steered Tom in the direction of the restaurant, just in time to see Jorge hobbling toward us, grabbing at his crotch. He stumbled to within a yard of me and reached for his groin again. He shifted his hips and something worked its way down the inside leg of his loose jeans. Jorge took another step and the mystery object clunked onto the sidewalk. Jorge looked down at the almost empty bottle of Mr. Dude, then back up at me with the goofy, big brown eyes of a child.

"Hi Val! Great to shee you!"

Jorge did a half-lunge, half-swan-dive at me. Tom stepped in and caught him just before he tackled me like a drunken linebacker.

"Hey buddy," Tom whispered gently to his former partner. "Probably time for you to call it a night."

Jorge nestled his head on Tom's chest and cooed like a dove. Tom looked over at Goober.

"Okay if Jorge bunks with you tonight, Sir Flatulence?"

Goober grinned. "Sure. I don't live far from here. Let me grab my tip jar."

GOOBER'S PLACE WAS nothing like I'd imagined it. The thing was, I didn't have to imagine it. It was *my* old place!

"What are you doing here!?" I demanded.

"Living," Goober replied dryly. "Keys in the mailbox? Not the brightest move, Val. Besides, the rent isn't due until the end of the month."

"I know! Because *I* paid for it through the end of the...aarrgh! Goober! Does the landlord even know that you're here? Oh my lord! He could come back from vacation any second!"

"Calm down," Goober said in a patronizing tone that made me feel anything *but* calm. "I've still got some cash. And like I said, I'm working now."

Goober poured the contents of the tip jar on the empty kitchen counter and pushed the assorted coins into piles.

"Three dollars and thirty-two cents." He scratched the top of his bald head. "That's like... eighty-three cents an hour."

Tom bumbled into the apartment with his old buddy slung over his shoulder, huffing and puffing from carrying Jorge up the stairs.

"What should I do with him?" Tom panted.

He eyed the place and managed a joke.

"Nice digs. Looks familiar somehow...."

"Cut the crap, Tom!" I shrieked. Panic rose in my throat, making my voice harsher and squeakier than I'd wanted. "They can't stay here!"

"What's the harm, Val?" Tom asked. "The place is empty. What damage can they do?"

I had no good comeback. *Dang it!* I sighed.

"Okay. You win, Goober. But I want you both out of here by morning. My name is on this lease!"

"Fair enough," Tom said. He looked Goober in the eyes. "Agreed?"

Goober slid the tip money into his pocket and shrugged. "Agreed."

Chapter Eight

I cruised by my old apartment the next morning to check on my squatters, Goober and Jorge. They were gone, just as Goober had promised, and had left the keys in the mailbox and the place in a decent state. I climbed back down the rickety wooden stairs with my broom, bucket and bottle of Ty D Bol unused.

Goober wasn't the only one getting the boot today. Lining the alleyway by the trash bins was an odd assortment of household trappings. A gutted vacuum cleaner, a pee-stained box-springs, a murdered side chair, boxes of jumbled clothes, and grocery sacks full of dirty, broken kids' toys. I fought the urge to investigate. During my unwilling incarceration in that tiny apartment, I'd born witness to anything and everything having been hauled over to and abandoned beside the bins in that alley. Back in my destitute days, I'd found some pretty good stuff amongst the rubble.

Old habits die hard. I was rummaging through a mangled box of clothes when my phone rang. The display screen read, "Unknown Caller." I answered it anyway.

"Hello?"

"Hello. Is this Valiant Fremden?"

Crap. The only people who used my real name were telemarketers and bill collectors.

"Who wants to know?" I said, instantly irritated.

"This is Police Officer Hans Jergen," said the stern voice. "I repeat. Are you Valiant Fremden?"

My snotty attitude slid into dread. "Yes. What can I do for you, officer?"

"I'm assigned to your case," he explained. "I need to interview you. When can you report to the station?"

"I already answered a bunch of questions the other day."

"That was just a preliminary. Are you going to cooperate?"

His impersonal, threatening tone made my stomach gurgle.

"Yes. Of course. When do you want to do it?"

"Does *now* work for you?"

"Uh, sure. Where are you?"

"At the police station, of course."

"Okay. Can you give me the address?"

"Good one. See you in ten minutes." He hung up.

I clicked off my phone, still stunned by the cop's flippant attitude. I wracked my brain. I'd driven by the police station countless times on my way to the beach. *Somewhere off 1ˢᵗ Avenue North.* I climbed into Maggie and turned the ignition. *Oh, yeah. Unlucky thirteen.* If I hurried, I had just enough time to get there within the ten-minute timeframe specified by Officer Jergen. From his tone, I figured I'd better make a good first impression. But somehow, I already knew I'd blown that opportunity.

SHOULD I CALL TOM? I fished my phone out of my purse in the passenger seat. I set it back down. I didn't want to add "dialing while driving" to any potential charges already on my list. I bit my thumbnail and turned right off Fourth Street onto First Avenue North. I passed the fancy, tiled arches of the open-air post office on the corner, then drove past nine blocks of buildings that grew more neglected with each

TWO CRAZY: BUST A MOVE

rotation of Maggie's tires. The old Ford's shocks groaned when I turned
into the parking lot on the corner of First and Thirteenth. *I* groaned
as I walked the gauntlet to the front door. I already felt guilty of something I couldn't name. I frowned, pushed my way inside and walked up
to the service counter.

"Hello," I said to the round-faced lady behind the glass. If she was a
cop or just a receptionist, I couldn't say.

"I'm here to see Officer Jergen, please."

"Which one?"

"Uh...*Hans* Jergen.

"Have a seat."

I eyed the row of battered, vinyl-seated chairs butted up against the
scuffed wall like a lineup of suspects. I sat in the least-victimized chair,
my purse on my lap, clutched in my vice-like grip. I waited ten minutes, dread growing with each odd-looking stranger that filed in and
out of the lobby. I studied them surreptitiously. *Murderer? Child moles-
ter? Thief?*

I'd worked myself into a state of angst by the time a guy wearing a
police uniform ambled up to me. His shirt matched his ice-blue eyes.

"Are you Valiant Fremden?"

It sounded more like an accusation than a question.

"Yes."

"Officer Hans Jergen. Come with me."

"Am I...under arrest?" I asked.

He turned his icy eyes on me. "*Should* you be?"

"No! I...I just don't know what's going on here."

"Just routine questioning. Nothing to fear. If you're not guilty, that
is."

If his words were meant to reassure me, which I doubted, they had
the opposite effect. I followed Officer Jergen into a small, eight-by-
eight room with a beat-up metal table and two hard, bare-steel chairs.
He motioned for me to sit in the chair furthest from the door. I gri-

maced. *I wish I had some Ty-D-Bol to wipe the chair down.* I swallowed, closed my eyes and lowered my haunches onto the seat that was still warm from the butt-cheeks of lord-only-knows who.

Officer Jergen didn't sit. He hovered, instead, like an angry ape, supporting his body on two white-knuckled fists. They pressed down hard on the metal table like frozen punches to the gut.

"So, Ms. Fremden, I recall from the report that human remains were found in your domicile."

"Uh. Yes. A finger to be exact."

His ice-blue eyes were mere slits, but I could still see they harbored something just short of menace.

"Would you say this is a common occurrence in your place of residence?"

"What? No!"

"Have you been involved in any other cases of missing persons, or missing body parts?"

"No!"

"I urge you to tell the truth *now*, Ms. Fremden. "Any lies will be uncovered during my investigation. That won't play well for you later."

"I'm telling the truth. I swear!"

My words sounded weak, as if I doubted them myself. A trickle of sweat slid down my back.

"So tell me. How did this finger come to be in your possession, Ms. Fremden?"

"It wasn't really in my possession...."

"You were the one to find it, correct?"

"Yes...."

"In your house, correct?"

"Yes."

"Then, Ms. Fremden, it was in your possession."

"Well, if you put it *that* way."

"I do. And I find it very suspicious that you would find a body part among your household furnishings. A couch, correct?"

I nodded. "But it was in the alley—"

"Yes, I've read your report," he barked, cutting me off. "Still, I find it highly unusual. Very convenient that the couch was out of your jurisdiction just long enough for someone to slip in a dismembered finger."

"Well, that's the way...it was." My voice faltered. I fought not to burst into tears. *Did he really think I was a criminal? What a jerk!*

"Who else had access to this couch at the time?"

My mind raced around aimlessly, like a headless chicken. *Was I supposed to know the answer? Three cats? A possum? A sleepy bum?*

"Uh...anybody who went down the alley, officer. That's what I was trying to tell—"

"For your information, finding a finger isn't, in itself, a crime, Ms. Fremden." Officer Jergen's jaw tightened to sinew. "But murder and dismemberment of a corpse is. No disfigured body has turned up as of yet. So I can't hold you. But you best be advised, I've got my eye on you."

I blinked hard and looked at the door to the tiny room.

"Can I...can I *go* now?"

"Like I said, I can't hold you at present. But that could change at any moment. You're free to go. But don't leave town."

I tried to stand but my knees buckled. A slight smirk curled the corner of Officer Jergen's lips. It reminded me of my German ex, Friedrich. A sickening, helpless feeling flashed through me, followed by a surge of determined hutzpah. I wasn't about to give this man the satisfaction of knowing he'd gotten to me. I took a deep breath and willed myself into Valiant Stranger mode. I set my jaw firm and stood up. I left ice-cold Officer Hans Jergen in that grimy little interrogation room without saying goodbye.

But then again, neither did he.

Chapter Nine

"Hans Jergen? That guy's a jerk!" groused Tom. *"He's* the cop assigned to the case?"

"Yeah." I stepped aside to let my good cop in the front door. "And I agree. He's a jerk, all right."

Tom took off his gun holster. "What did he do?"

"Well, nothing specific. He just acted like a jerk. Like he already knew I was guilty. He thinks I had something to do with cutting the guy's finger off. Maybe even killing him! He said he'd be waiting for a body to turn up. And that he 'had his eye on me, and I better not leave town.'"

"Crap." Tom put his gun and holster on top of the refrigerator, then opened the door and pulled out a beer. "Want one?"

"Yeah. Thanks. What's the deal with that jerk, anyway?"

"He's the son of the Chief of Police, Franz Jergen," Tom explained. He handed me a can of beer. "That makes him a real stickler for protocol. He's got something to prove, even if no one else cares but him and his uptight old man."

"Really?" I pulled the tab on the Fosters. "The attitude I got from him...well, it didn't seem like *protocol.* It seemed more *personal* to me."

Tom looked away and licked his lips. When he looked back at me he was biting down hard on his bottom lip. I knew what that meant. It was Tom's "I don't want to tell," tell.

"What is it, Tom?" I took a sip of beer and kept an eye on his face.

Tom blew out a breath. "He and I have some bad blood together."

"What?"

"Val, I don't make a habit of asking you for favors, but I'm asking for one now. Just let that answer be enough, okay?"

I WOKE UP DEAD TIRED. I'd slept alone, but Tom's secret had stayed the night and played ping-pong with my mind until nearly 3 a.m. It would've been so much better if he'd just told me a lie. At least then my restless mind would've had something to focus on. Instead, I'd found myself imagining all kinds of ridiculous scenarios. *Hans Jergen slept with Tom's ex-wife. No. Tom ran over Hans' dog. No. Tom and Hans were once lovers. No. Hans had an affair with Tom's dog....*

I'd never thought of Tom as a man with a shady past. With his meticulously ironed clothes and smooth-shaven good looks, I'd fancied him as a kind of blond Mr. Clean, wholesome inside and out. Not knowing Tom's "deep dark secret" ate away at my ability to think like a pitcher of Long Island iced teas.

I was in the kitchen trying to put together a grocery list, but even fortified with two huge cups of coffee, I couldn't get past item one—Ty D Bol. I recalled the time Tom had blindsided me before, when he'd neglected to mention that his "friend" at the forensics lab was his bombshell-gorgeous ex-wife. I wondered what else he had conveniently forgotten to clue me in on.

Arrgh! There was only one way to tame the vicious gerbil running circles to nowhere inside my skull. I needed some serious chocolate therapy. The big guns. It was time for a trip to Chocolateers.

I tore the one-item list from my notebook and slipped it into my purse. I ran a brush through my wavy brown hair, locked the front door behind me and slid sideways onto the red, fake-leather bucket seat behind Maggie's steering wheel. I turned the ignition and hit the gas. The vintage Ford's twin glass packs rumbled like a pack of angry, 'roid-raged bears.

DOWNTOWN ST. PETE WAS the kind of gritty-yet-trendy city center that suited both the ambitious *and* the artistic. Gleaming glass buildings towered over tiny, single-story shopfronts straight out of Main Street, circa 1930. Cracked sidewalks and red-brick alleyways led to walls adorned with amazing, hip murals, smelly dumpsters, and drunken derelicts. Chic new vegan restaurants sprouted up next to junk shops disguised as antique dealers, both doomed to die in the toxic fog of capitalistic disinterest. Still, somehow, one thing—no, *two* things—seemed to always prosper in any socioeconomic environment; coffee houses and chocolate shops.

Addiction was never short of admirers. I was living proof. My brain worked better with a caffeine or anandamide buzz, and I was Jonesin' for some chocolate, big time.

When I needed a coffee fix, Brew'delicious had my vote. I loved the friendly baristas at the cozy wooden bar and the homey, eclectic hodge-podge of couches and chairs where patrons could sit and sip as long as they pleased. But when it came to cocoa beans, I was pulled like a mating-season salmon toward the stream of dark, rich heaven known as Chocolateers.

Both shops were on Central Avenue. Chocolateers was closer to Beach Drive, wedged between an Irish pub and one of those new cigar bars that seemed to be popping up everywhere like pimples on a fat man's behind. Personally, I didn't get it. Cigar smoke was the best woman repellant ever invented. It wasn't as if the men frequenting those places needed *another* reason for women to avoid them.

As I walked by Cigar Daddy's, I was forced to pass one of their customers puffing it up at a sidewalk table. Rotund and revolting, the man could have run a comb through the hair growing out of his nose and ears. His mint-green Nehru shirt had reached maximum capacity long ago, and could no longer span the girth of his huge beer belly. As I walked by him, he nailed me in the face with a lungful of smoke that smelled like a cherry fart.

I stared at him in disgust. *Really?* My copywriter brain kicked in. *Come and get it, ladies! Fat, greasy, ham-fisted troll—now with extra stink!*

I battled my way through his miserable cloud of *screw you* and slipped inside Chocolateers.

If there really was such a thing as Nirvana or Heaven, it had better include chocolate or I'm not going. I felt my pupils dilate as I stared at the exquisite dollops of dark- and milk-chocolate delicacies arranged in precise rows and tidy boxed sets. Like puppies at a rescue center, I wanted to take *all* of them home with me. But like I've said before, I couldn't be trusted alone with chocolate.

"So, what's it going to be today, Val?" asked the thin man in a white apron and chef's hat.

"The usual, Jack."

I drooled over a stack of peanut clusters and debated whether I should be happy or embarrassed to be on a first-name basis with the proprietor.

"Two dark-chocolate-covered cherries coming up."

Jack reached a slim hand toward a stack of small, white paper bags, then hesitated. He looked over at me. His friendly face asked a question to which he already knew the answer.

"Just hand 'em over," I said.

I shoved a five-dollar bill across the counter.

Jack grinned. "Why do I always feel like a dirty drug dealer when you come in?"

I shot him a jaded sneer.

"Because you *are*, Jack. You're the gaul-dang chocolate pusher-man."

Jack nodded apologetically.

"Well, I have to admit it, Val. You *do* look like you just got a fix every time you pop those cherries in your mouth."

"You of all people should know, Jack. Great chocolate fixes everything."

I picked up the cherries. Jack watched me intently from the corner of his eye. He knew from experience that looking head-on at what was coming next would be too much for him to bear.

I crammed both chocolate-covered, liquid-centered globs of ecstasy into my mouth. Jack blanched. He waved goodbye and I slipped out the door. I concentrated on the yummy flavors as I ran past Cigar Daddy's and its patrons' smelly, yellow haze of disgust and desperation.

MEETING MY CHOCOLATE dealer had placed me just a few blocks from the convenience store-cum-drunkard's paradise called Detroit Liquors. During my first year back in the States, this humble little shop had earned a huge place in my heart. It was the only shop within walking distance of my old apartment, so it was there where I was first introduced to Fosters beer. Along with malt liquor, cigarettes and condoms, "The Deet" sold Fosters in shiny silver cans as big as my head. After seven years abroad, I'd returned home in need of a friend. Fosters had been the first one to meet my criteria; it was cheap, easy to get along with, and it never talked back.

My list of friends had grown a bit over the last year and a half. The party I'd thrown a few days ago was a good reminder of it. But it also put to mind the fact that I could use a few women friends. At any rate, my birthday festivities had me running low on beer and Tanqueray. I decided to walk down to The Deet and pick up a six pack and a pint.

I crossed the street and window-shopped the row of glass storefronts along the way. One shop advertised huge glass jars of olives and olive oil. Another window displayed gourmet cupcakes topped with spring flowers piped in bright green and yellow icing. Abby's Shabby Chic was crammed with old furniture painted white to look new, then the edges rubbed off to look old again.

Because it was designed near the turn of the century, every city block in downtown St. Pete was divided in half by a brick-paved service alley. I crossed the alley half a block from The Deet and looked up from my cellphone. A tall, bald guy was walking in my direction, pushing a baby stroller up the dumpster-lined side street. He waved. I took a closer look. It was Goober. I stopped and waited for him.

"What's up with the stroller?"

"Hitting all the known vices today, I see."

I eyed him with a tinge of suspicion.

"What do you mean?"

"Come on. Chocolate drool *and* The Deet?"

I frowned and wiped the corners of my mouth with the tips of my thumb and forefinger. Goober grinned and gave me a quick nod. My face was clean.

"Thanks. So, what are you doing with a baby stroller?"

"You mean BOB? I'm working on my next avocation."

"What happened to Le Fartomane?"

"Le Petomane," Goober corrected.

He shook his deeply tanned, peanut-shaped head.

"Tsk. Tsk. How soon the fartiste is forgotten."

I blew out a big sigh. "Well? Why did you quit?"

"I didn't. I got shut down."

Goober glanced up and down the alley. He leaned in closer toward me. He pushed down on the stroller until it creaked under his weight.

"Darn shame, too. I was just getting good at it. Yesterday some cop came by. Said he was getting complaints and that I was disturbing the peace. 'Unsanitary insanity,' he called it. Dirtbag! One little technical difficulty and I'm out on my butt." Goober blew out a big sigh. "Another budding career brought down by a bad burrito."

I blanched and recoiled involuntarily. I willed myself to think of rows of pretty chocolates, puppies playing in the park, even smelly guys with cigars—*anything* but the image trying to force its way to the surface of my mind like a beach ball trapped underwater.

"So what's with the baby stroller?" I asked yet again, desperate for a diversion.

"Guy's gotta make a living." Goober said.

"What about the money I gave you?"

"A pack of dogs ate it."

"By dogs, he means greyhounds," Jorge said from behind me.

I turned around. Jorge's hair and the aviator sunglasses on top of his head gleamed the same blue-black in the glaring sun. He appeared relatively sober, considering it was already almost noon. He shot me a rare glimpse in the eye, then studied my sandals.

"Greyhounds?" I asked.

"Derby Lane."

Jorge shot a glance at Goober. He smoothed his moustache with his thumb and forefinger, then wiggled his bushy upper lip back and forth, settling the hairy beast back in place.

"Yeah, yeah," said Goober. "Nothing to worry about, Val. I've got a new place to live and another idea in the works. See? I found this premo baby stroller in the alley. A BOB sport utility model. A beaut, isn't she?"

I eyed the stroller. It looked like an overgrown tricycle with handlebars over the back wheels. With its fat rubber tires, rugged stainless steel body and thick canvas seat, it appeared to have been built to withstand a lunar landing.

"It's the SUV of baby transportation," boasted Goober proudly.

"It's busted," I said.

"Yeah, the front axle's bent to hell," agreed Goober. "But Winky says he can fix it for me."

"What are you going to do with it, Goober? I hate to be the one to break it to you, but nobody's going to trust you with their baby."

"Don't be ridiculous, Val."

Goober shot me a look of pity for my pathetic ignorance.

"I'm talking about a *new* customer service here. Something totally outside the playpen, sore to speak."

"What are you talking about?"

"You know all those people you see pushing their dogs around in strollers?"

"Yeah."

"Well, I'm the new *dog* taxi. Specializing in pampered pooches. I was thinking about calling it Goober Dog."

I raised my eyebrows in astonishment. "That's so bizarre it might actually work."

"It better," said Jorge. "Goober lost all his money *and* his job on Beach Drive."

"Jerks. I wasn't panhandling. I was offering a legitimate entertainment venue in exchange for charitable donations."

I rolled my eyes. "I'm sure you can get your spot back."

"Venues aren't as easy to come by as you think Val. The busker community can be vicious. I'd been lucky that a place had opened up when it did."

"Who had it before?"

"Some guitar player, I think."

"What happened to him?"

Goober shrugged. "Who the hell knows?"

"Do you know a lot of guys out here, Goober? Panha...uh...buskers, I mean?"

"I'm making a name in the community. Why?"

"Well, I might need your help finding someone. The guy who helped Tom load my couch onto his 4Runner."

"Sure. What did he look like?"

"I...I don't know."

Goober shot me a wry look. "Well, *that* certainly narrows it down."

Chapter Ten

O f all the things I'd dreamed of doing when I was a little kid, toting around a picture of a dead finger wasn't one of them. Probably because I'm a girl.

Five days had passed since the cops hauled the crappy couch away to wherever they stored that kind of evidence. They'd told me I'd get the sofa back after the case was solved. I figured that was an excellent reason *not* to get involved in finding the finger's owner. But then that threatening interview with Officer Jergen had changed my mind. I could end up in hot water over that stupid thing.

I hadn't talked with Tom about the hobo napping on the couch yet, so all I had to go on was the souvenir photo on my phone. Tom had taken a snapshot of the disgusting digit right before he'd dunked it into the pickle jar he'd taken from my fridge. Someone at the party ate all my kosher dills and put the empty jar back. Given my guest list, it could have been anybody.

At any rate, a dismembered finger wasn't the kind of thing you could show just anybody. Thankfully, none of my friends were the prissy type. I was sitting in the corner booth at Water Loo's watching Goober, Winky and Jorge take turns ogling the gruesome picture on my cell phone screen.

"So, you guys have any ideas about whose finger it could be?"

Goober glanced at the picture again.

"The initials on the ring are W and H. Hmmm. Let me think. Oh! I know! It belongs to old Wanna Humper!"

Winky sucked in a chortle and snorted out a laugh.

"Another good'un, Goober! Mister Wanna Humper, let me introduce you to Anita Mann."

Goober slapped Winky on the back and they both laughed until tears streamed down their cheeks. *I guess rotten minds laugh alike.* Jorge either didn't get the joke or didn't think it was funny. Being the first cop on the scene of the traffic accident that had killed his wife and kids had maimed the poor guy for life. I handed Jorge my phone. He laid it on the table in front of him, then curled his fingers into binoculars and studied the photo, section by section.

"The guy had money," Jorge said into the table. His head was still down, his face a few inches from the picture.

"Sure. He had a gold ring," I said.

Jorge looked up, his half-lit face showing a clarity I'd never seen before.

"He also had a manicure. Trimmed cuticles. Nails buffed to a polished shine."

"You mean *nail*," Winky said.

He snatched the phone away from Jorge.

"It's only *one* lousy little finger, compar-do. Looks like his picker, too."

"That's gross, Winky!" I said.

"What's so gross about playin' guitar?" Winky asked. "Get yore mind outta the gutter, gal."

I LEFT WATER LOO'S in a better mood, my faith in my skid row pals renewed. Jorge had given me the first clue for my case. I called Tom with the news.

"Tom, your buddy Jorge came up with something interesting. He said the finger belonged to a guy who took care of himself. It was manicured."

"Uh huh. Good. Anything else?"

"He and Winky both agreed it was an index finger."

"Okay. So we're looking for a guy missing *that* finger. Right or left?"

Crap! "I don't know. I didn't think to ask. Hey, do you want to come by tonight? I want to talk to you about the hobo."

"Which one? Winky or Goober?"

"Ha ha. The one that was sleeping on the couch. Who helped you load it into your truck."

"I know. Look, Val. He was just your average derelict. About five-foot eight. Full head of brown hair. Probably mid-forties."

"Any distinguishing characteristics?"

"Look at you, miss fancy detective."

"I'm just doing my best to stay off the radar and out of jail. Can you think of anything?"

"Hmm. Well, he had a bunch of tattoos. But who doesn't nowadays?"

"Remember any of them?"

"Yeah. He had a mermaid tail on his left arm. Her head was on his neck, getting ready to bite him like a vampire. His t-shirt covered up the rest."

"Are you kidding?"

"Yes."

"Come on, Tom! This is serious! Don't you care about me clearing my name?"

"Sure I do. Just trying to lighten you up. Okay. Seriously. He had a scar across his right cheek. And a chipped upper front tooth. Left, I think."

"What color were his eyes?"

"Not sure."

"What color are *my* eyes?"

"Crap brown."

I didn't say a word. Tom had hurt my feelings. *Again.*

"Anyway, I can't come over tonight, Val. Something's come up."

"Okay. Bye."

I clicked off the phone, my heart a jumble of conflicting emotions. *Why had Tom treated my situation so casually? Why had he insulted me? Why didn't he want to come over? Was Tom breaking up with me? Is that why he didn't buy me a birthday present?*

Chapter Eleven

I spread my arms and legs like a starfish across my full-sized bed, lifted up a butt cheek and let one rip. I sank back down into the mattress and sighed. It was nice not to have to entertain a one-man audience tonight. I was in a foul mood, and I wanted to enjoy it in peace.

Alone time was definitely underrated. Tom and I had both been married before. I'd found the whole situation grossly overrated. "*Til death do us part,*" sounded like a terminal sentence. I much preferred Tom's and my arrangement; "*Til space do us need.*" Somehow it just...*worked.*

Sprawled out in my bed alone, I distracted my racing mind by staring at a crime investigation show on TV. I could always count on the narrator's droning voice to put me to sleep....

I dreamt I was locked up in a facility for the criminally nude. Each of my fellow inmates roamed the hallways in some state of disrobe. Those on the road to recovery from wanton nakedness wore random bits of clothing. One had on a shoe. Another, a floppy hat.

I was seated in a long hallway. A big black guy wearing a single sock walked by. Next came a red-headed woman wearing a bra and panties. She looked at me and shook her head scornfully. An old man wearing a kilt danced a jig and sang a song, the words to which I couldn't make out. I watched him intently as he passed.

When I turned back around, I discovered a short, thick man standing in the hallway, just two feet away from me. I could see his toenails.

They looked like talons. The man's face was obscured by an eagle mask. It was the only thing he wore besides a single glove...a glove with one missing finger. He tapped me sharply on the shoulder with his left index finger.

"You're it!" he squealed.

He turned and ran down the hallway, his butt cheeks bouncing with each hard footfall. I tried to chase him, but I couldn't. I was tied to the chair, completely naked. Apparently, I was incorrigible.

I WOKE WITH A START.

"What the hell!" a voice said.

I squinted at the clock radio. The blurry, glowing letters sharpened into 3:13 a.m. I'd forgotten to turn it off.

"Where the f#@% is it?" the voice said.

My sleepy brain began to fire off a few neurons. *Wait a minute. You can't say that word over public airwaves.* An ice-cold shot of liquid fear surged through me. I sat up in bed like a rocket.

"What the f#@% did you do with it?" demanded a man's muffled voice from somewhere in the darkness.

I closed my eyes and shook my head. *This had to be a dream.*

"I said, where the hell *is* it?"

The voice was louder. Closer. The bottom corner of the mattress sank down from the pressure of someone's body weight. My blood turned to ice water. The clock cast a dim green glow on the shadowy silhouette of a person in dark clothes and a Halloween mask, sitting on the bottom corner of my bed.

"I'm not here to hurt you, lady. I'm here to find.... What the...! Just tell me. Where's the freakin' finger?"

The finger! "I...I don't have it. The...cops. They took it."

My fumbled words sounded strange and far away.

"The *cops!* Blast it all to hell!"

The intruder punched the bed with his fist. Like a spectator, I watched, fascinated, as my right leg reared back and kicked the man square in the mask with the butt of my heel. He tumbled off the bed in a noisy heap.

"Aaughh! Mother of macaroons! My eye!"

"Get out!" I screeched. "Get out of here!"

Screaming used up my last drop of adrenaline-fueled bravado. I backed up against the headboard, yanked my legs into my chest, pulled the covers to my chin and waited in the silence for whatever might come next.

The man gathered himself off the floor with a grunt. He limped out of the dim room, a trail of obscenities following behind him. I sat, frozen in my seated fetal position, until I heard the front door open and shut again. I tried to reach for my phone, but my arm wouldn't cooperate. By the numbers on the clock, it took eight minutes for my body to start working again. When it finally did, I reached numbly for my cellphone and punched #7. Speed-dial for Tom.

"Tom!" I croaked. "Robber...couch...finger!"

"Val? Are you all right?"

"I...I...."

"Just calm down. I'm here. I'm listening. Are you okay?"

The sound of Tom's voice loosened my tight lungs enough for me to get some air.

"Yes. I think so. Just...freaked...out."

"What happened?"

"Someone broke in!"

"What!"

The full force of what had just happened hit me like a punch to the gut. My hands began to shake. My throat felt dry and stretched. I dropped the phone. My fingers were stiff and clumsy as uncooperative as I fumbled to pick it up again.

"Val? Val? Are you there?"

"Yes..."

"Is he still in the house?" Tom's voice was restrained panic.

"No."

I heard Tom let out a big breath.

"Okay. Good. Stay calm. Did he hurt you?"

"No."

Another big sigh of relief from Tom.

"Did he steal your purse? Cash?"

"No. He wanted the finger."

"What? You said he was after *the finger?*"

"Yeah. I told him the cops had it. He got mad and punched the bed. I...I kicked him and he left. Oh, Tom, please, can you come over?"

"I'm sorry, Val." Tom's voice shifted to professional detachment. "But this is getting into serious territory. As much as I hate to say it, you're going to have to report this to Hans Jergen. He's probably going to do a crime-scene investigation."

"Can't you come anyway? Just to *be here* with me?"

"I want to, believe me. But my presence wouldn't help your case."

"What do you mean? Why not?"

"I told you, just trust me on this, please."

"Wait a minute! *My case?*"

"SO LET ME GET THIS straight, Ms. Fremden," Officer Jergen said dryly.

He stood in my kitchen, his left ankle crossed over his right, and shook his condescending head scornfully at his police report.

"A man broke into your house last night and asked where your finger was."

"Yes. Well...no."

I was still in my bathrobe, my hair tangled, my face strained with shock.

"I don't think it was *my* finger he wanted. I think he was after the *other* finger."

Officer Jergen looked up from his report, his ice-water eyes pierced me with suspicion.

"Did he ask specifically about a *severed* finger?"

"Um...no, but what else could he have meant?"

I looked around my little house. Two cops were milling around. My beautiful, fresh paint job was being covered in black splotches of fingerprint dusting powder.

"Ms. Fremden, pay attention," Officer Jergen scolded. "You say this man was about four feet tall, wore a George W. Bush mask, and spoke mainly in obscenities."

"It could have been an Alfred E. Neumann mask...the *Mad Magazine* kid? It was dark."

Officer Jergen scribbled on his report. "Noted. Then you kicked him in the face and he ran away."

"Exactly."

"Ms. Fremden, we have found no evidence of forced entry. No evidence of a struggle, either. In fact, no evidence at all to corroborate your story. Right now, it's just hearsay...*your* testimony against a theoretical...*trick-or-treater.* Tell me, do you take prescription medication of any kind?"

My bleary eyes showed their bloodshot whites. "What? No!"

"Do you take any other types of drugs, legal or illegal?"

"No!"

"An almost empty pint of Tanqueray gin was found in your freezer. Were you drinking last night?"

"Well, I had a nightcap. A Tanqueray and tonic. But that doesn't mean I—"

"Ms. Fremden, given the gravity of human dismemberment cases, defendants have been known to concoct cover stories to point law enforcement down blind alleyways."

"But I didn't—"

Officer Jergen cut me off again. This time, with his icy eyes full of disgust and contempt.

"I have to say, a cussing, finger-thieving, dwarf president of the United States is one of the more imaginative stories I've heard in a while."

Jergen coughed out a cynical laugh and shook his head.

"Mother of macaroons? That's a good one."

I stared into his cold, humorless face. "But it's the truth!"

"According to *you*, Ms. Fremden, But I don't believe it. Who would? I was going to let this case go. But in light of these events, I'm more convinced than ever that you're hiding something. If you're going to lie, at least try to do it well. I suggest you tell your absurd story to someone who has a vested interest in believing it."

"What do you mean?"

"Ms. Fremden, I suggest you hire an attorney."

Chapter Twelve

*C*rap! *Crap! And double crap! Just when I thought my life was getting back on track, I go and get the finger from the universe. And now I need an attorney.*

Again!

The only lawyer I knew in Florida was J.D. Fellows, my dead parents' estate attorney. When the last cop left my place at 9:30 a.m., I called Mr. Fellows' office and made an appointment with his secretary for 10:15 the next morning. After I hung up, I got out a sponge and a bucket of water and went to work on the fingerprint dust encircling my walls like a dirty bathtub ring.

At least there was one thing I could always count on. Ty D Bol. After an hour or so, I'd removed most of the fingerprint powder. But the fragile, shaky feeling that had enveloped me in the wee hours of the night still clung to my back like a cold, damp rag. For the first time since leaving Germany, I felt unsafe. Worst of all, I wasn't sure which man was the most to blame for it—the masked intruder, hateful Officer Jergen, or my fair-weather boyfriend who *didn't* come to my rescue.

There was only one sure-fire way to lift my mood when it was this low. I showered, pulled on a pair of jeans and a tank top, turned the ignition on Maggie and headed in the direction of Chocolateers.

IT WAS WEDNESDAY MORNING all over again. I was still savoring the sickly-sweet aftertaste of cherry cordial and dark chocolate when I spied a familiar silhouette heading toward me. This time, it was hard *not* to notice Goober. He sashayed down the sidewalk on Central Avenue with his freshly patched-up moon-lander stroller. Twist-tied to the front of it was a makeshift cardboard sign that read: *Über-Dog Royal Pet Services.*

Long, lanky Goober dressed for his new career in an oversized blue t-shirt, black cut-off shorts, purple tights and orange Converse high-top sneakers. On top of his shiny bald head, positioned at a rakish angle, was a Burger King crown with a bone-shaped doggie treat dangling from the front-most spike.

I didn't even cringe. A worrisome thought crossed my mind. *Maybe this is my new normal.*

"How's the new job going, Goober?"

The mustachioed king of the canines shrugged.

"Actually, as they say in the biz, Val, pretty doggone crappy. I think people may be more persnickety about their pooches than they are about their own kids."

"You could be right. Yesterday I saw a poodle in a stroller wearing a freaking rhinestone tiara. The owner gave her a sip of Evian from her own water bottle."

Goober lifted his crown and wiped the sweat from his bald head. He eyed me suspiciously.

"Chocolateers *again*? Okay, now I'm worried. You all right, Val?"

I hung my head a little and smiled wistfully.

"I've been better."

"What's up?"

"I've got a mean cop on my butt."

Goober's eyebrows shot up an inch. He leered at me and started to say something, but I cut him off.

"And I don't mean Tom."

Goober's eyebrows returned to normal. He held out his hand for me to shake.

"Oh. Well in that case, let me officially welcome you to the club."

BEFORE I LEFT, I GAVE Goober the lowdown on Tom's description of the alley hobo. No one had risen immediately to the top of his beer-soaked mind, but he'd said he'd keep an eye out for a guy with a scarred cheek and a chipped tooth. I also gave Goober my phone number and ten dollars to top off his pay-as-you-go cell phone so we could keep in touch. It was the first time I'd given one of the three derelicts my phone number. I hoped I wouldn't live to regret it.

I passed a garage sale sign on my way home. It triggered another one of Valiant Stranger's weaknesses. Maggie squealed as I hooked a hard right and followed the yellow, hand-drawn signs to a tiny little purple cottage with a detached garage almost as big as the house itself. The garage door was open and lined with tables and bookshelves heaped with junk. A chubby redheaded woman sat in a lawn chair in the driveway. She had a money belt around her waist, a clear-green plastic visor on her head, and a bag of Cheetos in her hand.

I felt like Gretel being lured into her gingerbread garage. Still, I couldn't fight my natural instinct to thrift shop.

"Howdy. Lookin' for anything in particular?" the lady asked as I walked up the drive.

"Not really. Nice setup you've got here."

"Thanks. Keeps me outta trouble and in Cheetos. Want some?"

The woman held up the bag and showed me her orange teeth.

"No thanks. I'll just look around."

"Help yourself. Holler if you need me."

I wandered through the garage. It was packed to the gills with the same things you find at every yard sale. Unused sporting equipment, ugly heirlooms, Avon collectibles and suspiciously unclean kitchen gadgets. I was just about to leave when I saw a box in the corner labeled, "Anything for 50 Cents". I took a peek inside and grinned. I handed the lady five bucks.

"Aww, I'm glad those things are going to a good home. You collect 'em, do you?"

"Yes. They bring me a lot of joy."

"Well I'm glad to hear it. Want me to wrap 'em in newspaper?"

"No. That won't be necessary. But thanks."

The woman handed me back three Cheeto-stained one-dollar bills. I put them in the plastic grocery bag along with my prizes.

"You get these often?" I asked as I walked toward Maggie.

"Pretty regular. Stop by and see me. I'm here most days."

"Okay, thanks. I just might take you up on that."

I slid into the bucket seat and carefully laid the bag on the passenger seat. As I rumbled toward home, four chipped ceramic figurines clinked together, gossiping amongst themselves in their China voices about how lucky they were to find a new home. They had no idea what they were in for.

Chapter Thirteen

On the ride home from the garage sale, I realized I didn't have a single girlfriend. Clarice, Berta and Glad...they'd all slipped away, like sand through my fingers. *Was I like that lady on* Murder She Wrote? *Everyone who came near me ended up dying. Well, the women, anyway.*

I sighed. I couldn't do anything to change the past. But I *did* have a shot at changing the future. Last-night's break-in had delivered more than one kind of shock. It was a rude awakening *and* a wake-up call. *I was repeating the same mistake I had with Friedrich; I was becoming way too reliant on Tom.* I needed to change that—and quick.

I wracked my brain. Was there a single woman I could turn to for friendship and advice? I thought about calling my adoptive mom back in Greenville, but I could hear her voice without even picking up the phone:

"I tried to tell you, Ragmuffin. But you're too highfalutin for my advice now. That's what happens when you go traipsing off to places you don't belong."

I hit the gas and headed toward home.

I WASN'T THE KIND TO burn bridges. It was more my style to neglect them instead. I'd mastered the technique while I was away in Germany all those years. Out of sight, out of mind, I'd banished my old ac-

73

quaintances to some cobwebbed corner of my brain. I'd paid little attention as my connections with my family and friends in Florida had grown weed-infested, corroded, and inched their way toward total disrepair.

Since my return a year and a half ago, these half-forgotten folks had begun to spring to mind again like snippets from a favorite movie. I'd already tried to reconnect with a few old friends, but I'd done so with guilty trepidation. And a bit of shame. After all, in their eyes (and maybe mine, too) I was a failure. I'd left the States riding a gallant, white steed of high-flying dreams. I'd returned dragging a dirty blue suitcase weighed down with painful lessons from the German school of hard knocks.

I'd lost more than a husband in Germany. I'd lost my best friend, Clarice. And fun-loving old Berta, too. Finding Glad passed away on her lounge chair last year had left me gun-shy about investing my heart with anyone I thought could truly hurt me. My puny little birthday-party guest list was undeniable evidence of how small I'd allowed my world to shrink. But lately, I'd begun to miss the company of old friends. And by "old" I meant the kind of friends I'd had *before* I'd gone abroad. The kind who didn't consider dumpster diving a valid career opportunity.

One such friend had been Milly Halbert.

Over eight years had passed since I last saw Milly. We'd been fairly close before I left for Europe. But I'd abandoned her like a pirate's wench when I sailed across the sea in search of *la dolce vita*. I'd returned nearly broke, with no job, no credit, no place to live and no friends that weren't either strange or estranged. I'd been snubbed by a few old acquaintances, and it had hurt. But I was sick and tired of licking the wounds from my personal shipwreck. I was ready to try crossing one of those old bridges again.

Being an admitted coward about all things relationship, right after I'd bought the figurines, I'd looked up Milly's number and texted her a simple note asking if she wanted to meet at Nitally's for lunch at noon. I'd gotten a one-word reply. "Okay." Not sure what to read into those four little letters, I'd turned Maggie around and headed back toward downtown. At two minutes to twelve, I placed a trembling hand on the restaurant door. My stomach rumbled from nerves and hunger. I was either going to get a hug or an earful of obscenities. I braced myself for the worst and pushed through the restaurant door.

"Valiant! Great to see you!" Milly hollered at me from across the restaurant as soon as I peeked in the door.

As it turned out, the worry had been for nothing. Milly Halbert was the unsinkable Molly Brown in my Titanic boatload of former friends. The sound of her voice and the sight of her heart-shaped face sent a delicious wave of soft, warm comfort washing over me. My eyes watered with gratitude. I smiled guiltily. Milly had been the only person I'd let call me Valiant, the weird name given to me by my adoptive parents. She'd earned the privilege. Her first name was even worse than mine.

"Millicent!" I shouted back. The sandy-blonde fashion diva winked a hazel eye at me, and, just like that, the eight years separating us vanished in the curry-scented air.

"There ought to be a law against men wearing sandals if their toenails look like Fritos," Milly half-whispered as I sat down in the red plastic booth opposite her.

She grimaced and bobbed her head sideways in the direction of the man sitting at the table next to us. Against my will, I took a peek. Milly's description was more accurate than I wanted it to be.

"Ugh. He ought to run a diet club," I said. "There went my appetite."

Milly giggled, then involuntarily snorted like a piglet. The old, familiar sound was as comforting as a warm blanket on a chilly morning. I drank it in. It felt good to be accepted as I was, despite my huge, gaping flaws.

"It's so good to see you again, Milly. Thanks for agreeing to see me."

"Are you kidding?" She winked again. "I'm grateful you texted. You're one of my favorite mistakes, my friend."

I grinned. Ironically, though Milly accepted me lumps and all, she offered no such slack to men unlucky enough to cross her path. In fact, when it came to the opposite sex, Milly had a list of offending "laws" as long as the bridge to Key West. This was one of the reasons I found her so endearing—and probably the main reason she rarely ever got a second date.

It certainly wasn't her looks that turned men off. Both Mother Nature and Father Time had been kind to Milly. She looked pretty much the same as she did last time I saw her. In a word, *gorgeous*. Blonde, slim, button nose, hazel eyes and the perfect height of five feet, five inches.

Milly was the kind of woman so outwardly perfect that a girl couldn't be blamed for secretly hoping she harbored some inner, hideous flaw, like psychopathy—or both sex chromosomes. But I knew better. In fact, over the years, the only flaw I'd ever detected in Milly was that when it came to men, she was ruthless and clueless. She attracted guys like lint to a black suit, but she couldn't seem to navigate her way around the inner workings of a relationship to save her life. Fed on a steady diet of reality shows and fashion-magazine dating advice, Milly seemed fated to strut the catwalk of life forever a stray.

"Well, Milly, if I'm one of your *favorite* mistakes, I can't be *that* bad."

"I'm serious! I've missed you, Val. Sometimes I think you're the only one who ever really *got* me."

"Sometimes you've got to *give* to get," I said with way more preacher in my tone than I'd intended. Dating Tom had me feeling a little smug. Maintaining a long-term relationship with a man was the only category in which I had the remotest chance of topping Milly, so I considered it remiss not to revel in it for just a second or two.

"But *getting* is so much better than giving," Milly whined.

She laughed at her own joke and reached toward me, accidentally knocking over her glass of water. I'd forgotten what a klutz she could be. The commotion caused Frito Toes to look our way. He shot Milly a lewd expression that should have stayed locked behind bedroom doors—or maybe jail bars. I watched as she turned away from him and faked a retch. *Classic Milly.*

She leaned over the table toward me.

"There ought to be a law against leering in public."

"He can't help himself, Milly. There ought to be a law against looking as good as you."

Milly laughed and brushed aside my compliment like biscuit crumbs from a tablecloth.

"Like I said, Val, I've missed you. You've been back what...a year? What have you been up to, naughty runaway?"

"This and that. You remember my mom?"

Milly turned up her nose. "Yeah."

"Turns out, she wasn't really my mom."

"I could'a told you that."

"What do you mean?"

"Sorry, Val, but that woman wasn't *anybody's* mom. Not the way a mother *should* be."

"Wait, don't tell me. There ought to be a law against mothers like her."

Milly smiled and cocked her beautiful, blonde head.

"Well, natch."

I grinned. "Let's see. I also moved into a house in Bahia Shores. I inherited it from my real parents."

"Wait a minute. *Real* parents? I thought you were kidding about your mom."

"No. It turns out I was adopted, sort of."

"Really! How did you find out?"

"That's a long story for another day. I'll fill you in over drinks sometime."

"Okay. But do you like them? Your real parents?"

"They're both dead."

"Oh. Dating anybody?"

Good old Milly. She was to romance what roads were to Rome. All her conversations led back to men.

"Yes."

Milly leaned in, her hazel eyes wide and sparkly. "Tell me about him!"

"Here."

I clicked my phone to a picture of Tom and slid it across the table. "He's a cop."

Milly grabbed my phone like it was a free diamond tiara.

"Woo hoo! What a looker!"

She glanced up at me, her eyes full of mischief.

"Did you meet him in jail?"

"Ha ha," I said dryly. "Thanks, Milly. Do I look that desperate to you?"

Milly laughed. "No. It's just that...meeting a nice guy is so... *freaking frustrating*."

"Lord knows that's true. How about you? Dating someone?"

Milly rolled her beautiful, long-lashed eyes.

"No. If I like them, they don't like me, and vice versa. I signed up on MatchMate last November. It's been what...five months now online? I've gone out with probably fifty guys. All 'one-hit wonders.' I tell you what, Val. Chemistry is a witch. A witch who must be obeyed."

"Geez. If *you* can't get a good guy, Milly, what chance do the rest of us have?"

"Honestly, Val! The cute guys are players. The smart guys are nerds or doughboys. The rest are *Duck Dynasty* contenders or potential serial killers. My new car's navigation system took care of the last reason to even *need* a man anymore. When my Pleasure Pony dildo arrives in the mail, I'm thinking of taking this baby off the market for good."

I hitched my lip up on one side. "I know it's bad out there."

"Bad? Last Saturday I spent all this time and money getting ready for a date. Manicure, pedicure, Brazilian, the works. This jerk showed up in a raggedy-ass Grateful Dead t-shirt and cammo shorts. I wouldn't have worn that outfit to wash my own car!"

"You don't wash your own car."

Milly shot me a look. "That's beside the point! You know what I did?"

"No. What?"

"I went back to my bedroom and changed into sweats and flip flops. I put my hair in a ponytail, marched my butt back out to the living room and said, 'I'm sorry. I didn't realize we were going to clean out your garage.'"

"You left your makeup on?"

"Of course! I'm not *that* stupid."

"Okay. Well, what did he say?"

"That's just it! He didn't say *anything*. He thought it was a joke. He *laughed!*"

I thought about Tom and his ironed jeans and non-Frito toenails. "Not all men are like that."

"I sure hope you're right, Val."

A metal chair leg scraped noisily across the concrete floor. The Frito bandito was making his getaway. As he passed us, he smiled and dropped a crinkly scrap of paper on Milly's side of the table. After he disappeared out the door, Milly poked at the crumpled note with a straw, as if it were contaminated with anthrax. She maneuvered it around until she could see the message scrawled on it. She read it out loud.

"Call me. You won't regret it. Steve."

"See? You're still attracting them like flies, Milly."

"Yeah. Buttcrack flies."

Milly's lips twisted into a tortured pout. She pushed the scrap of paper off the table and watched it fall to the floor. When her eyes met mine again, her mouth had morphed into a devilish grin. She scrunched her head to her shoulders.

"With toenails like his, he's probably got a foot fetish," she teased.

The game was on again.

"Eeeww!" "Okay. I've got one," I said. "I wonder if Mr. Fritos comes with his own bean dip."

"Gross!"

I dropped my voice an octave and leered at Milly. "Drop your drawers my lovely and join me in my hot tub full of bubbling brown goop."

Milly reached across the booth and slapped me playfully on the shoulder.

"Aauughh! I forgot how good you were at this. You win. I'll pick up the tab."

"You don't have to, Milly. Let me. I'm grateful that you showed up."

"Rules are rules, girlfriend. Speaking of which, there ought to be a law against making someone picture that guy in a hot tub."

"True enough. I'd be the first to second that motion."

I DECIDED NOT TO TELL Milly about my predicament with the finger. Not yet, anyway. It'd been so wonderful to see her again. I didn't wanted to scare her away. *Hi! Haven't seen you in years! You look great! Me? Oh, nothing special. I'm just the main suspect in a human dismemberment case.*

After lunch with Milly, Tom had called. He'd wanted to come over tonight. I'd lied and told him I had a headache.

The truth was, I was still hopping mad about him leaving me to deal with the break-in and Officer Jergen *all by myself*. To top it off, he *still* hadn't bought me a birthday present. I'd tried to be a big person about it, but my giant wad of hurt feelings had grown so huge it finally out-weighed even my fear of falling victim to another home invasion. I'd acted nonchalant with Tom on the phone, and secretly taken a perverse pleasure in the notion that if I got murdered tonight, it would be his fault. Tom would have to live with the guilt. *Forever.*

Resentment clotted into a throbbing, grapefruit-sized knot just above my heart. The only thing saving Tom from my wrath was my foolish Southern pride. It was time for a full-on pity party. I poured down more than a couple of TNTs and lined up my adorable garage-sale figurines on a concrete block out in the backyard. I plopped into in a lawn chair and watched the sun disappear. In the fading twilight, I took a hammer and smashed the four porcelain cutie pies into a million dusty bits.

Chapter Fourteen

Last night's "knick-knack-give-a-whack" therapy worked. I woke this morning in a better mood. I made myself a cappuccino and basked in soft, sunny memories of a dream I'd had about Glad. She'd been sprawled out in her pink lounge chair in the sugar-white sand next to Caddy's beach bar, grinning at me from underneath her Gilligan hat, her drawn-on eyebrows arching over black, bug-eyed sunglasses. She got me longing for a nostalgic trip to Sunset Beach. I googled the news. Still nothing about the finger. I guessed the coast was clear.

I slipped on a bathing suit and was halfway out the door when a thought stopped me and shoved me back inside. *Crap.* I had an appointment with J.D. Fellows at 10:15. Anxiety barged its way inside my mind and shattered my mellow mood like a cheap figurine.

"SO, JUST TO BE CERTAIN I have this correct, a very short man dressed as either George W. Bush or Alfred E. Newman broke into your place in the middle of the night, sat on your bed, and demanded to know where your finger was?"

"Well, when you say it like that, it sounds kind of weird."

"We don't say weird here, Val. We say *implausible.* So, how short was the man?"

I averted my eyes. Even though J.D. Fellows towered above me in his special chair positioned strategically behind his custom mahogany desk, when he'd ushered me into his office, he'd been eye-level with my elbows. Despite the fact that our relationship stretched a bit beyond professional, in his office sanctum Mr. Fellows was all business. His question about the height of the perpetrator sent my political correctness radar skittering off the charts.

"Um...well, first he was on the bed. Then I kicked him. He flew off of it. And then he ran away."

Mr. Fellows remained silent and stared at me dubiously through the bifocals on the end of his bulbous nose.

"It was dark. It was hard to tell."

"Can you be more specific? Did you perhaps see him near some familiar item by which you could compare his height? A nightstand or doorway, perhaps?"

"Yes. That's how I knew he was short."

"Yes, we've established that he was short. Now we need to know *how* short."

"Um. Exceptionally short. You know what I mean?"

Mr. Fellows raised a sarcastic eyebrow. My face flushed red.

"Short like me, you mean?"

"Um. Yes."

"And the finger? Do you think it belonged to...the man in the mask?"

"No. It was a full-sized finger."

"My dear, we 'short people' can have full-sized body parts."

"I...I didn't mean to imply—"

"You know I practice estate planning, Ms. Fremden. I'm not a defense attorney."

"Yes, I know."

"So why did you come to *me*?"

Crap on a cracker! My carefully steered conversation was careening off a cliff. Mr. Fellows looked like a tea kettle ready to blow.

"Well. I thought you might know—"

"Look here, Ms. Fremden. Just because I'm a little person doesn't mean I know every single one of them on the planet! It's not like there's a Lollipop Guild of St. Petersburg or something!"

"No! No! I meant...that I thought...you might know...*an attorney.* To refer me to."

Mr. Fellows deflated like a leaky balloon.

"Oh. Well. In that case I—"

A voice buzzed over Mr. Fellows' phone intercom, interrupting him mid-sentence.

"Mr. Fellows! Mr. Greene is on the line. He says it's an emergen—"

Mr. Fellows clicked a button on the phone, silencing the intercom. He reached a hand across the desk in my direction, but didn't make eye contact. I shook it and let it go.

"I think that will do for today, Ms. Fremden. I will call around for a referral for you. I'm not used to dealing with criminal cases."

"Thank you."

"I trust you can see yourself out?"

"Oh. Yes. Of course."

I wanted to apologize, but feared it would just make things worse. I opened the solid, mahogany door to his posh office and stepped out. As I turned to close the door behind me, I took a last peek at Mr. Fellows. He wasn't hiding his feelings anymore. He was red-faced angry, and began yelling into the phone. I closed the door behind me carefully, as if to not wake the sleeping baby. But this baby was not only awake. Its diaper needed changing.

I LEFT MR. FELLOWS' office feeling like I'd stepped in every cow patty in a forty-acre field. Was the whole world angry at me? Out to get me, even? I needed a shoulder to cry on. I didn't want to wear out my welcome with Milly, but she was the only shoulder I knew of that didn't reek of sweat and booze. I took a chance and texted her about meeting me for lunch at noon at Ming-Ming's, my favorite sushi place. I got a text back that read: "Natch!" I grinned, jumped in my old Ford and headed west on Central toward the beach.

I'd just pulled into a parking spot at Ming Ming's when my phone chirped. I answered it. A familiar, baritone voice was on the line.

"Goober One to Goober Two."

I groaned.

"Hey Goober. What's up?"

"I got a fella here says he knows a fella."

"Okay. And?"

"Says the scar-faced kid is called Capone. Pretty clever, eh?"

"Extraordinarily creative."

"Don't be a sourpuss, Val. It's busker society rules. Never use your real name. We all have our handles. You know. Code names."

"I get it. So what does this guy know?"

"Liar Lewy? He says Capone hangs out mainly in the area around Seventh and Second. That's his territory, sore to speak."

"How did Liar Lewy get *his* nickname?"

"How the hell should I know?"

"Well, it doesn't add to his credibility factor."

"I guess. But that's what he says."

"Thanks, Goober. So what's your code name?"

"Wouldn't *you* like to know."

Goober clicked off the phone. I wasn't sure if he'd hung up on me or his phone had run out of money. I hauled my sad butt out of my car and took a table inside Ming Ming's to wait for Milly.

Chapter Fifteen

As usual, Milly had men on her mind. So between bites of Ming Ming's sushi, I brought up my troubles with Tom.

"I don't know, Milly. I mean, I like being someone's partner. But I also like sitting around the house with no pants on. And being able to fart whenever I want to."

Milly giggled. "Uh oh! Do I detect the shining knight's armor starting to rust?"

I sighed and my shoulders slumped.

"I dunno. That's a good question. I mean, we always want what we don't have, right? You don't have a relationship and *want* one. I've *got* one, but now I'm not so sure I *want* it."

"It's the never-ending 'catch twenty-two', Val. Don't get me wrong. I like my single life. But if I was in a relationship...married, I mean...I'd feel so much *safer*. My future would be secure."

"You're kidding, right? I've been married three times. There's no security in it! Not in *my* experience, anyway. All I ever got out of marriage was a case of emotional schizophrenia."

"What do you mean?"

"I dunno. I guess I just could never figure out how to stay true to who *I* was and what *I* wanted. I always turned into some strange version of whoever the hell I thought *they* wanted me to be. It drove me nuts!"

Milly eyed me playfully with her sparkling hazel eyes.

"I can see that."

"Ha ha. Anyway, sorry for the tirade."

"Don't be. Val, you're like the black widow spider of relationships."

"Eeew. What do you mean?"

"Nothing is wasted. When you're done with a man, you eat him alive."

"Gee. Thanks."

"No, I mean it in a good way. You dissect him. Digest him. Get all that you can out of the relationship. Learning wise, I mean. Not like me. I just keep repeating the same mistakes."

"You and me both, sister. I feel like I haven't learned squat. I'm more like the earthworm of relationships."

"What?"

"I can't tell which end is up and I keep digging new holes for myself."

Milly laughed.

"At least they're *new* holes."

I smiled sarcastically.

"So tell me, Milly. What's *your* latest mistake?"

Milly's eyes brightened.

"I call him refrigerator man."

"Cold?"

"Not exactly."

"Square?"

"No. Just the usual. Clueless."

"Okay. Spill it."

Milly leaned in, her eyes sparkling. She lived for moments like this.

"I met him at a bar. We danced. He was short, but kind of cute, you know? So I gave him my number. He texted me, asking if I was busy the next evening. I texted back I was free. He texted the word 'good' back, but by five the next afternoon, I still hadn't heard a word."

I shook my head in girlfriend sympathy. I knew what came next couldn't be good.

"Typical."

"Right? So I thought, forget this crap. I called a girlfriend and we went to dinner. So, it's half past seven and I'm halfway through my salad when this guy pings me. One word. 'Wazzup.' Then he sends me a picture of his freaking refrigerator!"

"Huh?"

"*Exactly!* I text back that I'm out with someone. He texts the word 'Later' and I never hear from him again. *W-T-F, Val.* What's up with that?"

"All I can say is, count your blessings, Milly. You nipped this jerk in the bud. It usually takes me seven to fifteen years to figure out a guy's a total jerk-wad."

Milly shrugged. "I guess you're right."

Milly's eyes glanced to the right. I could almost see the lightbulb go off over her head.

"There ought to be a law against a man parting his hair down the middle."

My eyes followed hers. Seated against the wall was a skinny guy in his fifties. He wore blue jeans and a red, silky-looking shirt emblazoned with a long-stemmed white rose design that wrapped around his ribcage and bloomed on his left breast pocket. He was busy studying a Ming Ming's menu through a pair of red bifocals. A greying mop of wavy hair parted in the middle hung down in his eyes. It looked like a geriatric Pekinese was taking a nap on his noggin.

"Do you think it's a wig?" I whispered.

"Gawd! I hope so!"

We both giggled. The game was on, and I was at bat.

"Hey. The seventies called. They want their shirt back!" I sniggered.

"Hasn't he ever seen like...*a fashion magazine?*"

"Or have *a friend* who's seen a fashion magazine?"

We were on a roll. Milly cupped her hands into a megaphone.

"Hey mister. Did you pay for that haircut or were you ambushed by a three-year-old *chimpanzee?*"

Tea shot through my nose. I ducked down and Milly snorted. I grabbed a napkin and held it over my nose and mouth as we both giggled and grunted and tried to regain our composure. When I could breathe again, I took my turn.

"Okay, okay. I got one. Hey dude! Are you related to Willie Nelson? 'Cause it's definitely time to get—"

"On the road again!" we exclaimed together.

We couldn't fight the tsunami and fell out, swamped with laughter. In the middle of our giggling fit, Milly knocked over her jasmine tea. The warm, brown liquid spilled across the table like an unfortunate bowel elimination and collected in puddles on the floor. I wiped tears of laughter from my eyes with my napkin, then bent over to sop up the spilled tea. As I did, I knocked heads with Pekinese man.

"Ouch!" I cried out.

The man jerked back and rubbed his head.

"I'm sorry," he said. "I was just trying to help out."

He held a tea-soaked napkin in his hand. Good old Southern guilt washed over me like a spilt baptismal pool.

"Oh. I'm sorry, too. Thank you," I offered sheepishly. "That's really nice of you."

"No problem," he said. "It looks like disaster's been averted. Anything else I can do for you two?"

I fumbled around for something to say. Milly was no help. She sat across from me, red-faced and silent as a guilty, naughty child.

"Um. Could you take our picture? I want one for—"

"Sure! You two get together and I'll peel off a shot."

I handed the man my cell phone and joined frozen-faced Milly on the other side of the table. The guy took a couple of snaps and handed me back the phone.

"Thank you," I said. "What's your name?"

"Nope."

What an odd name. I expected him to return to his table, but instead, the man made his way toward the exit door. Milly and I watched him as he opened the door and stepped outside. As the glass door slowly shut behind him, he turned to us and spoke.

"Have a nice day, ladies. I make it a policy to never get on a first-name basis with jerks."

AFTER MY LUNCH HUMILIATION, I figured I might as well stay in the gutter. I left red-faced Milly paying the check at Ming Ming's and drove east on Central Avenue. I hooked a left at Third Street and drove into the alleged hangout of scar-faced Capone.

The red brick streets of the Old Northeast neighborhood were rutted by monsoon rains and a hundred years of vehicular traffic. Maggie hated them, and so did I. To save her from damage, I parked along Second Street, a block away from Old Northeast Tavern. The place was probably Florida's first attempt at a strip mall. Built in the 1930s, it suffered from Spanish flat-roof design and American lack of commitment. Its merengue-like stucco façade and three-story clock tower had faded to an orange-pink hue from decades of standing in the glaring, tropical sun. The five-store lineup of tiny businesses within it came and went with the tide—just like the rest of Florida's transient population.

The only establishment that had demonstrated any staying power against this fickle, economic outflow was a pizza joint offering pies by the slice. Being three blocks from my old apartment, I'd eaten there a few times last year when I'd been in desperate need of a pizza fix. Even though the name of the place lacked originality, Old Northeast Pizza's pies didn't. They were delicious. And the price was right—$2.50 for a slice as big as my head.

As I walked along the sidewalk across the street from the strip center's row of shabby storefronts, I spotted a guy with a chipped tooth fishing pizza crusts out of the wastebasket outside. It looked like my growing street smarts were paying off. I patted my inner Valiant Stranger on the back.

"Hey. Are you Capone?" I called from across the brick street.

The guy jumped and poised for takeoff like an Olympic track star. He looked my way and I saw his scar. *Bingo!*

"What a ya want?" he yelled back. His voice was hard, but curious.

"Nothing. You helped a guy load a couch onto a 4Runner about a week ago. Right?"

Capone shrugged. "Maybe. Maybe not."

He put a crust between his teeth and ripped off a hunk. I walked across the street as he eyed me warily like a hungry raccoon.

"Look. I just want to know if you stuck anything in the couch. For safekeeping. While you were napping on it."

Capone stopped chewing the crust. He fished a cigarette butt out of his mouth, looked at it, tossed it in the trash bin and commenced to chewing again.

"Anything like what?"

"Like a finger? With a gold ring on it?"

"Are you outta your mind?"

"I'm not accusing you of cutting—"

"Lady, if I found a gold ring, do you think I'd *load it onto a truck and watch it drive away?*"

He had a point. *Dang it. There went my best lead.*

"Okay. Thanks Capone. Here's five bucks for your troubles. There's plenty more where that came from for the right information on the finger. Either who lost it or who's looking for it."

Capone snatched the fiver from my hand, then looked over at the pizza place. I took a step back in the direction of my car.

"Hey lady. How am I supposed to get a hold of you? With more information, I mean?"

Brilliant, Val. Some detective you are. I didn't want to give another derelict my number, so I gave him Goober's.

"Just call this guy. You probably know him already."

"Who is he? A cop?"

"No. A friend of mine. Bald. Bushy moustache. He pushes a stroller sometimes?"

"Not ringin' any bells."

"He's got a head shaped like a peanut?"

Recognition flashed across Capone's face.

"Awe, yeah. You mean Bushwacker."

IT WAS A GORGEOUS AFTERNOON in early April, and I didn't feel like going home. I took a nostalgic stroll by my old apartment, hoping the fresh air would clear my head and help me think. *Who could have put that finger in my couch?*

Florida didn't have seasons. Not like most people thought of them, anyway. April was the closest thing to autumn that St. Pete had to offer. It was the time of year when the live oaks shed their tired old leaves all at once. Within the span of a week or so, the huge, old trees transformed themselves almost as drastically as caterpillars turning into butterflies.

Massive canopies of olive-green leaves died overnight and their tannish-brown carcasses rained down like snow onto lawns and cars and streets and swimming pools. Within a day or two, the shiny green leaves that had pushed the old leaves off unfurled and formed massive, neon-green umbrellas against the blue sky. Then the oaks set about sprouting male and female flowers. If pollinated, the female flowers hung tight and turned into acorns. The male flowers, or catkins, had no such chance. They released their pollen, shriveled up and came careening down to earth. Their crumbly, wormlike bodies fell by the millions and collected on sidewalks in drifts, like dust bunnies under a bed.

I shuffled along the cracked sidewalk half covered in oak leaves and catkins, and counted my blessings that I wasn't allergic to oak pollen. I crossed Beach Drive and breathed in the sweet fragrance of jasmine in bloom. It hung from the wrought-iron fence of one of the mansions that lined the block between Beach and Northshore Boulevard. Across the street was Northshore Park, an oasis of green grass dotted with oaks and the occasional exotic Poinciana or Jacaranda tree.

The city park's east side ended at a concrete seawall. I found a bench in the shade facing the wide expanse of Tampa Bay. Seagulls screamed and blue jays quarreled with each other as I sat quietly, waiting for some inspiration that would help get me off the hook for finding that horrid finger.

How did that dwarf guy know the finger was at my place? And why on earth would he want it back so badly that he'd broken into my place?

One thing was for sure; it had to be someone who knew the couch belonged to me. That's the only way the dwarf could have known *I* had it. *Unless...*he or one of his buddies was in the alley when Tom and Capone loaded the couch into his 4Runner. They could have been hiding there, waiting for Capone to get off the couch so they could retrieve the finger. Yes. It could have been someone watching from the alley who followed Tom to my place.

Geez. If that was the case, it could have been anyone.

Chapter Sixteen

Tom spent the night last night. He ran the sink while he was in the bathroom, driving home the fact that we were still in that tense, awkward phase all new relationships went through. We were both still clinging to the illusion that we were perfect. Even so, old habits each of us had swept under the rug were beginning to crawl their way to the surface. He left the cap off the toothpaste and the toilet seat up.

Being on one's best behavior was a hard act to maintain, and we were beginning to tire under the strain. This morning, after some half-hearted cuddling and a couple of cappuccinos, I went to the kitchen and googled the crime-related news for St. Petersburg. It had sort of become a compulsion of mine ever since my interrogation by Officer Jergen. I kept waiting to open the screen and learn that the police had made an arrest in the case. But there hadn't been a word. Not even a report about me finding the finger. I was dying to know what was going on, but I didn't dare mention it to Tom. Every time I'd tried, he'd shut me down. He refused to get involved.

I closed the laptop, opened my mind to some dirty thoughts, and snuck back to the bedroom and my handsome, law-enforcement lover. As I peeked around the doorframe, my jaw hit my toes. Tom was already dressed, standing over the bed. He had my cell phone in his hand and was swiping at the screen. I nearly tripped over myself.

"What are you doing with my phone?!"

Tom jumped and dropped the phone like it was a chunk of lava. It landed on the bed upside down. Tom's sea-green eyes scanned the room, searching for an alibi.

"Nothing, Val. I thought it was mine."

He bit his lower lip. He was lying.

"Oh. I didn't know you had a pink case on your phone, too."

"It was dark in here. I just switched on the light."

"Well, then. What did you write down on that piece of paper?"

"This?"

Tom held the scrap up, but kept the blank side toward me.

"Just a buddy of mine's...uh...birthday. I mean address. I wanted to send him a birthday card."

"Oh."

Tom walked over and kissed me.

"I've gotta go. Call you later today, okay?"

I looked him in the eye, but I couldn't read him.

"I'm not done talking about this."

"Okay, but not now. I've got to go."

Tom slipped on his shoes and was out the door in under thirty seconds flat. I watched him drive away, then clicked the power button on my cellphone. The picture of me and Milly at Ming Ming's came up. I'd told Tom about Milly last night over dinner, but I hadn't shown him her picture. She was way too gorgeous, and probably just his type. Was it her number he'd written down?

I needed a chocolate fix, big time.

I set the phone down and opened my bedroom closet. I rifled blindly through the rack, searching for a sundress to slip into, but my mind couldn't focus on the task. I stopped and let my arms drop to my sides. *What the hell was Tom up to?*

I'd counted on Tom to be honest with me. I'd thought he was totally trustworthy. He'd helped me move in. Helped me renovate. I'd even given him a key to my place. What was going on? I sighed. Maybe he was telling the truth. Maybe he had just been mistaken.

The thought of losing Tom made me miss Glad even more. After she'd died, I'd discovered Glad had stored her life away in shoeboxes. I'd taken a cue from her and begun doing the same. My photos and mementos and important papers were tucked away in a dozen shoeboxes on the top shelf in my bedroom closet. I'd lined my boxes up neatly, based on type of shoe. Smaller sandal boxes were on the left, then high-heel cartons, then walking-shoe boxes to the far right. I wondered if I'd have to start a new box soon....

I found the blue denim dress I was after. I tried to pull it out, but it was tangled on another hanger. I yanked harder, but it hung on like one of those hook-armed apes from a Barrel of Monkeys.

Arggh! I was on my last nerve. I jerked the hanger so hard the head snapped off and sent me tumbling butt-first to the floor with my dress in tow. *Perfect.*

I was just about to snap the rest of the hanger in half when something caught my eye. I stared up into the closet from my position on the rug. The hair on the back of my neck pricked up. My tidy little collection of shoeboxes were all mixed up.

PEOPLE WITH OVERACTIVE imaginations like mine should never be left alone too long with their untamed thoughts. We're apt to concoct outrageous scenarios that make the truth, once revealed, nothing more than a disappointing footnote. I hoped that would be the case with Tom's dirty little secret involving Officer Jergen, and whatever else he might be up to.

For some reason, Tom had begun to not share things with me. This new void in his trust had reignited a familiar, unwanted, defensive edginess inside me. All my life I'd been bitten hard on the heart by men and their secrets. I didn't want to be played for a fool again. It was high time

I learned to watch my back. I made a mental note to pay closer attention to what Tom was up to.

MY ARMS WERE CONTORTED behind my back, trying to zip up my denim sundress, when the phone rang.

"Goober One to Goober Two."

Men! "Hello, Bushwacker."

"Crap. Who told you that?"

"Who do you think?"

Goober yelled, but not at me.

"Capone, I'm gonna kick your butt!"

A distant voice called back, "Not if I kick yours first!"

"Goober! Calm down. Why are you calling?"

"I got Capone here. He says he knows who belongs to that finger you found."

"Who?"

"He won't say without pay."

"How much does he want?"

"Your standard rate. A fiver."

"Well, give it to him. I'll pay you back."

"I don't carry that kind of money around on me. I could get bushwack...*crap!* I could get *robbed.*"

"Okay. Tell him to stay there. I'll be right over."

I hung up, grabbed my purse and ran out the door. I jumped in Maggie and made a beeline down Gulf Boulevard. I hooked a right on First Avenue South, the main drag to downtown. Then I realized I didn't know where I was going. I hadn't asked Goober where he was. *Dang it!*

I swallowed my pride and clicked redial. Goober answered in a smart-alecky tone.

"Goober One to Goober Two. Forget something, Goober Two?"

"Just tell me."

"The pizza place where you met him last time. Capone only agreed to wait if you added a slice of pepperoni to the ante. I made an executive decision."

"Okay. Good work, Goober One."

I could hear him smile over the phone.

"You're welcome, Goober Two."

I clicked off the phone and saw flashing blue lights headed in my direction. *Aww crap! Just what I need. Another cop on my butt.*

I pulled over. A policeman climbed out of his car. It was Officer Jergen. *Double dang it!*

"Ma'am, you know you were going forty-five in a thirty-five? Oh. It's you."

"Yes. Hello Officer Jergen. Nice day, huh?"

"It *was*. License and registration."

I handed them over.

"Val Fremden. You know Fremden means stranger in German, don't you?"

"I've been told, yes. I take it you're German?"

"American with German ancestry."

"Oh."

"Any more problems? Break-ins, I mean?"

"No, but I'm working some leads, trying to find out whose finger it was."

"Are you a detective?"

"No. Not exactly."

"Then do all of us in law enforcement a favor, Ms. Fremden. Don't go messing in police business. You could end up in more trouble than you already are. Take my advice and leave it to us to handle your case. I suggest you drop whatever it is you're doing."

I shot him my best smile.

"I will if you will."

He looked down and started writing in his ticket book.

"Nice try."

BY THE TIME I ARRIVED with my $128 speeding ticket in tow, the guys had finished their slices and were being held for ransom by the young guy working the place.

"There she is!" Goober shouted and pointed at me. "That's her over there!"

I walked across the brick street to the open door of Old Northeast Pizza. A brawny young man with a man bun and more tattoos than a Navy base eyed me doubtfully.

"These two belong to you?" he asked.

I grimaced. "Yes."

"Good thing. Another minute and I was gonna call the cops. Last time I give out a slice up front."

"Sorry for the inconvenience. What do I owe you?"

"Seven bucks even. They both got the lunch special. A slice and a soda."

I handed the man a ten dollar bill.

"Keep the change. Sorry for the trouble."

The young man's tough-guy façade melted like butter in a microwave.

"Hey, thanks! Well, all right then! You guys are good by me. Go ahead and untie 'em."

Goober and Capone both reached down and began to unkink the wad of knots in their shoelaces that bound their feet together. I tried not to smirk.

"So, Capone. Who's the guy with the finger?" I asked.

Capone stopped untying his laces and looked up.

"You mean without the finger."

"Yeah."

"Let me see the money."

Five dollars? What is this? L.A. Vice meets Candid Camera? I fished a five out of my wallet and handed it over.

"Name's Mickie Harden. We call him Hard-on."

Goober slapped Capone in the back of the head.

"This here's a lady, Capone. Mind your manners."

I smiled at Goober. "Do you know where we can find him?"

Capone hooked a thumb in Goober's direction.

"You might better ask Bushwacker here. Hard-on used to play guitar for tips downtown. After his little 'accident,' Bushwacker here took over his spot. He's the only one I seen that gained something outta Mickie not being able to play no more."

Goober glanced up at me. "I don't know the guy, Val."

"Sure you don't," Capone sneered.

"Hey! Capone! Play nice," I said. "Can you get word to Hard...to Mickie? Tell him that I'd like to talk to him?"

"Maybe. For the right price."

"Can you get him here for fifty bucks?"

"Lady, for fifty bucks, I can get you the pope."

Chapter Seventeen

I was some kind of hapless weirdo. I lived in two parallel, yet diametrically opposed dimensions. On one plane of existence, I was just good-old Val Fremden, your typical, late-forties, Caucasian woman. Southern. Brown hair. Average build. College grad. Nothing remarkable about my appearance or intellect. On another plane, I was my alter-ego, Valiant Stranger, an aspiring, bumbling gumshoe wannabe with a cadre of known associates I quite often wished I *didn't* know. In the weird, twilight space in between, where these two dimensions collided, lived Glad's daughter, Thelma Gladys Goldrich—the universe's favorite victim of circumstances.

Why in the world did that finger have to end up in my *couch?*

I pondered this question and a few more over a Tanqueray and tonic. *Was Capone telling the truth? Was the finger Mickie's?* If it *was* the guitar player's digit, I was off the hook for potential homicide. But if Capone was truthful about *Mickie*, did that mean he was right about Goober, too? *Did* Goober know more than he was telling? Had Goober actually cut off Mickie's finger? No. I couldn't believe that. At least I didn't want to believe that I could believe that. And now, to top it all off, Tom was acting suspicious. He was the one who'd hauled that ugly-ass couch into my house in the first place. Why would he have done that if he wasn't in on this whole scheme, too?

Geez! Could things get any more complicated?

The phone rang. "Unknown Caller." I took a slug of TNT and clicked the green button.

"Hello?"

"Ms. Valiant Fremden?"

My mood went from bad to worse

"Yes, Officer Jergen."

"I'm calling to inform you we found the body."

I sat bolt upright, suddenly cold sober.

"What?"

"A body has been found in a dumpster near downtown. It's been deceased for about three weeks, and is missing most of its fingers. It looks like a match. And a possible homicide. Is there anything you would like to add to your statement now, or do I have to call you in for questioning?"

"I told you already. I didn't do it. What about the dwarf? The fingerprints?"

"Analysis of the fingerprints taken at your house yielded no foreign prints. I assume Officer Thomas Foreman was there earlier, assisting with the removal of the finger. That's why his prints were found. Or do you have another explanation?"

"No. No other explanation."

"Uh huh. I thought as much. I'll be in touch. Don't leave town."

Officer Jergen clicked off the phone. I poured another drink and picked through my DVDs. I pulled out *Sense & Sensibility*.

"You were right about men, Jane. They're complicated."

Chapter Eighteen

I guess fifty bucks went a long way in the world of the down and out. I'd just finished googling the news and pulling the rest of my hair out when the phone rang.

"Goober One to Goober Two."

"Hey, Goober."

"Got Capone and Mickie here behind The Deet. I can hold 'em if you pay for a pint."

"Yes! Sure! Great work, Goober. I'll be right there."

I clicked off the phone and scurried around like a deranged rat. I yanked a clean shirt from the closet and buttoned it, then played hide-and-seek with the house for my favorite jeans. I found them in the dirty-clothes pile. *Crap.* I glanced around to make sure my mother up in Greenville wasn't looking. I grabbed the dirty jeans out of the heap and pulled them on. I inched into some flip-flops and was out the door in under a minute.

I was cruising down Gulf when my phone rang again.

"Ms. Fremden? This is attorney Marvin Hemingway."

"Uh...yes?"

"Mr. Fellows said you needed representation on a defense case?"

"Oh! Yes. But no. Not anymore. I think I've got this covered."

"Yes. Right. Well, keep me in mind."

"Look, I'm driving," I said. "Thanks for the call, but I've got to go. Goodbye."

I clicked off the phone and headed east on First Avenue South. I hit the gas, then caught sight of something sticking out of the glovebox. It was the corner of that blasted speeding ticket. I eased off the gas and prayed for the lights to stay green. Of course, I hit every red after that.

I was waiting for another light to turn green when my favorite radio show came on. The folks at WTFM, "That's For Me" radio had a hilarious program that replayed drunk-dialing disasters, funked-up phone-ins to the station, and inane, inebriated messages left on people's answering machines.

"Jack Hammer here! It's nine o'clock, friends and fiends! You know what that means. It's time to get down and dirty with the latest edition of *Blurs & Slurs.*"

I turned up the dial. A drunk guy was stammering out a sentence between hiccups.

"Hello?...(hic)...Is this the...(hic)...What The (bleep) Station?"

"Yes sir. It certainly is. What can we do you for today?"

"I gotta...(hic)...boner to pick with you guys."

"Sorry sir. We don't play that way."

"Huh? I thought...(hic)...you played anything."

"What would you like us to play, sir?"

"I forget. Hey, is this the...(hic)...International House of Pancrakes?"

"Oh, yes it is! What would you like to order?"

"Bacon. Kevin likes lots of bacon. And Jack Dan—"

I found a parking spot a block from The Deet and switched off the ignition.

"What a dope," I said to the radio.

I fed the meter with quarters I'd saved from when I used to have to go to a laundromat. Thank goodness I didn't have to face that sweaty social humiliation anymore. I walked to the alley behind The Deet. Goober, Capone, and a tall, skinny guy with red frizzy hair were passing around a pint of Mad Dog and bickering like three wet hens. It was as if I hadn't turned the radio off. It was *Blurs & Slurs* live and in color.

"You already had four swigs. It's *my* turn," Capone bellowed at Goober.

"I didn't realize you could count to four, Capone."

"Hand me that bottle," said the third guy.

The red-headed guy reached for the bottle of whiskey with his right hand. His left hand was covered in a dirty bandage. He and Goober played tug-of-war for the pint of rotgut. I interrupted their game.

"Goober? What's going on?"

Goober let go of the bottle, sending the frizzy-haired dude careening against the wall of a building. He dropped the whiskey bottle. It shattered on the red bricks.

"Now look what you've done, numbskull!" Capone groused. "You can't do nothin' right!"

Frizzy hair reared back his bandaged hand and was about to whack Capone in the face with it when Goober grabbed his arm.

"All right, gentlemen! Calm down."

Oddly enough, at Goober's command, the two men straightened up like schoolboys headed for a paddling. I was impressed.

"Ma'am, this here's Mickie," Capone said. "He's the one missin' the finger. You got the money?"

"Yes," I said. "But first I need some information."

"Show me the money, first," Capone said.

I sighed. "Sure."

I pulled out two twenties and a ten from my wallet and waved them in the air. Capone's eyes followed them like a kitten watching a feather on a string.

"Okay," he said.

I turned to Mickie. "How did you lose the finger?"

"Uh...on a saw. I was working construction."

"Okay. How did it get into the couch?"

Mickie looked over at Capone.

"What's she talking about? *What couch?*"

Goober stepped up to Mickie.

"Let's see it," he demanded.

Capone and Mickie glanced at each other again.

"See what?" Mickie asked.

"Take off the bandage," Goober said. "Let's see it."

"I don't wanna," Mickey said. "It's...uh...unsanctified."

"Unsanitary, you idiot!" Capone yelled.

Capone backhanded Mickie's bicep. Goober lost his patience.

"Do it now, or I'm gonna knock both of you out cold!"

I'd never seen peanut head truly angry before. It scared me. *If they start a brawl, what the hell am I going to do?* I took a step back.

"Okay, okay," Capone said. He turned to Mickie. "Just do it."

Mickie unraveled his bandage. All five fingers were alive and well.

"I wasn't lying," Capone said. "The guy you want is Mickie. I just couldn't find him."

"So who's this guy, then?" I asked.

"Someone who wanted ten bucks."

I turned to Goober. "How did you know they were lying?"

"Come on, Val. Look at the guy. Construction work? That guy couldn't lift a hammer to nail a fly to the wall."

CRAP, CRAP, CRAP! Now I had nothing to prove my innocence. And I still didn't have an attorney, either! Where could I go from here? I climbed in Maggie and was halfway back to the beach when I realized I'd forgotten to go to Chocolateers. Boy, I really *was* in deep. I glanced over to my left as I passed my favorite restaurant. I forgot all about fingers and chocolate and possible jail time. In the parking lot of Ming Ming's, sidled up next to Tom's silver 4Runner, was Milly's red BMW.

Chapter Nineteen

I nearly lost control of Maggie.

What were Tom and Milly doing together? WTF? Was it just a coincidence? Or were they having an affair?

It took all the strength I could muster not to turn Maggie around, go flatten their tires with a butcher knife, then march into Ming Ming's and knock their feeble heads together like two rotten coconuts. *What the hell was going on, here?*

When it came to confrontation, I talked a good game. Safe within my own thoughts, I could devise all kinds of dastardly ways to exact my revenge. But in the end, I never did any of them. I'd learned a long time ago there was no real joy in it. Besides, what if this really *was* just an innocent coincidence? I'd have made a jerk of myself. And even if it wasn't, what right did I have to interfere? Tom and I weren't engaged. We never even discussed *monogamy*. I guess I'd just assumed....

Aunt Patsy's snippy, self-righteous voice filled my head. "When you *assume* you make an *ass* out of *u* and *me*."

Screw that!

I hit the brakes, did a one-eighty in the middle of Central Avenue and set my sights on a whole new kind of investigation. But the closer I got to Ming-Ming's, the more my rage turned to uncertainty. By the time I'd driven the six blocks back to the restaurant, my self-righteousness had lost most of its steam. I settled on a sensible stakeout instead of a crap-slinging showdown. I turned left and parked a block away, on the opposite side of Central. I crept back and crouched behind a car parked at the laundromat across the street. Peeking out from behind the rusty bumper of an old Ford Bronco, I had a clear view of Ming Ming's. I crouched down and rehearsed my interrogation lines.

I didn't get much practice. A minute later, Tom and Milly came out, all insipid grins and giggles. Tom pressed something into Milly's hand and kissed her on the cheek. She laughed. He opened her car door for her and she climbed in. Tom walked around the back of her Beemer to his 4Runner and fiddled with the door. A strange thumping sound filled my ears and everything turned red. My mind melted into a pile of infuriated mush.

I jumped up from behind the Bronco. I drew in a big breath in preparation of projecting a stream of obscenities across the road. But before I could make a sound, my phone rang.

Was it Tom? The lying, cheating jerk himself?

I shut my hang-dog mouth and squatted back down behind the car. I squirmed with anger like a trapped weasel as I fished around for my phone. I couldn't make out the caller I.D. All I could see was stars.

"Yes? Who is this?"

"Goober One to Goober Two."

Crap! "What do *you* want?"

"Hello to you, too Miss Manners."

"Sorry. Look, Goober, I'm kinda busy. What's up?"

"Too busy to meet the *real* fingerless freak?"

"What? Another one? Does Capone have them lined up in the bushes? I don't have time for another wild goose chase."

"It's not. This is the guy."

"How do you know it's the right Mickie this time?"

"Let's just say, 'I checked.'"

As I pondered that for a second, a loud voice rang out behind me.

"Lady, what are you doing?"

I turned to see an obese black woman in a tight pink dress eying me like I was Lizzie Borden. She held her cellphone in her hand like a weapon.

"Get away from my car or I'm calling the police!"

I stood up just in time to see Tom's silver 4Runner driving away. Milly's car was already gone.

Crap!

"I'm leaving, okay? Geez!"

I brushed off my knees. The woman kicked the air.

"Go on, now. Git!"

I took a few jogging steps in the direction of my car and put the phone to my ear.

"Goober? Are you still there?"

"Yeah. And I thought *I* led a weird life."

I WAS BACK AT OLD NORTHEAST Pizza, springing bail for Goober, Capone, and if peanut-head was right, the *real* fingerless Mickie. He was short fellow, not any taller than me, with a mangy grey ponytail that hung like a faded, weather-worn rope halfway down his back. Apparently, Mickie was in the habit of losing body parts. His once-handsome face was now punctuated with a gold front tooth, a goatee to match the rat tail, and a patch over his left eye. He, Goober and Capone were busy chewing mouthfuls of pizza when I walked in. Goober gave me a salute. I nodded back.

"What are the damages?" I asked the tattooed pizza guy.

"Ten-fifty."

"Here's fifteen. Could you add a slice to it? I'm starving. Plain cheese, please."

"No problem."

The pizza guy put a slice on a wooden paddle, shuffled over to the pizza oven and slid it in. I turned my attention to the trio of derelicts in front of me. Mickie held out his four-fingered hand, the stump where his index finger used to be was still red and scabby. I shook his hand and tried not to retch.

Great. I have to eat pizza with this hand.

"I'm Mickie," he said. "I hear you found my finger."

"See? I told you I'd find the right guy," Capone sneered. "Where's my fifty?"

"Shut up Capone," Goober said. "You'll get your money when my friend here's satisfied this guy's the real deal."

Capone eyed Goober, then looked at his paper plate.

"You gonna eat that crust?"

Capone reached for it. Goober swatted his hand away. Capone scowled and got up off his stool. He stuck a finger in the coin return of the pin-ball machine next to his chair. It was empty. His face soured again and he plopped back down on his stool and sighed.

"Yes, Mickie, it looks like I did find your finger. I'm curious. How did you lose it?"

Mickie eyed me warily.

"I didn't. Somebody took it."

"What do you mean?"

"Somebody cut it off."

"Why would they do that?"

"I dunno. Maybe I owed 'em money. I got a few debts outstanding."

"Like you, lady," Capone groused. "You owe me fifty bucks."

Goober swatted Capone on the back of the head.

"But why would they take your finger? It's not worth anything—is it?"

Mickie eyed me with curiosity, then concern.

"It was for the ring. They couldn't get it off.... Hey! Wait a minute. It was *you!*"

"*Me?* What are you talking about?"

"*You* did it. You and your boyfriend. You jerks rolled me when I was drunk. You put a sack over my head. I couldn't see your face. But I'd recognize your voice anywhere. You told him to do it!"

"Do what?"

"To cut my dang finger off!"

"What? You're wrong! You've got the wrong person, Mickie. I'm trying to—"

"Trying to what? Get my gold tooth next? Stay the hell away from me!"

Mickie jerked to standing and ran out of the pizza place, his ratty ponytail trailing in the air behind him. Goober and I stared at each other, stunned. Capone held out his hand.

"Harummm."

I placed two twenties and a ten in his dirty little palm.

"Here's your pizza," the tattooed guy said.

Capone shoved his money into his filthy jeans and eyed the slice.

"You gonna eat that, lady?"

THE SKY WAS FALLING. I went home and hid under my bed. No matter which guy the finger belonged to, I was totally screwed.

Chapter Twenty

Something crawled across my face. I shot upright and smacked my head, hard.

"Ouch!"

In the grey twilight, swarms of dragonflies thronged around me. My head pounded and my mouth tasted of dust. A plastic, monocle-wearing peanut grinned at me from under its black top hat. I sat up in the booth on one elbow and touched the tender bump on my forehead. I scowled at my two assailants, an overhead kitchen cabinet and an empty bottle of Tanqueray. I'd spent the night with them and Glad in her old RV.

I vaguely recalled getting home yesterday. Then the memories came flooding back like a clogged toilet. A crazy man was after me for cutting off his finger. A crazy girlfriend was after my lying boyfriend. A crazy-mean policeman was after me for murder. And *I'd* been crazy enough to think getting plastered would solve everything.

I sat up and grunted as I reached down to the scuffed linoleum floor. I picked up Mr. Peanut. Hot tears sprang from my eyes and thumped onto his monocle eye, making it appear as if he were crying, too.

"I miss you, Glad."

A tear rolled down Mr. Peanut's pitted cheek. I held the bank to my chest and whispered to my dear, departed mom.

"What would *you* do if you were me?"

"I'd get off my duff and get a shower."

The voice came from a small window above my head. I turned around and looked up. Laverne was smiling and waving at me.

"Rough night, Val?"

"Kind of."

"One night you're pulverizing porcelain, the next you're camping out with a piggybank. What's up with you?"

I sniffled. "Same-old-same-old."

"Aww. Come on, sugar. Tell me about it over a cup of coffee."

"Have you got a bra on?"

"Ha ha! No. But neither do you."

I looked down. I was wearing one of Tom's t-shirts and a pair of his boxers. *Geez. I must have gotten way drunker than I thought.* I stood up. My head thumped like a bass fiddle. I sniffed away my tears and pouted at Laverne.

"It had better not be decaf."

WHILE LAVERNE POURED the coffee, my eyes poured over her décor. Laverne's house was a museum of Vegas memorabilia. Her white leather couch was covered in playing-card pillows—red hearts and diamonds, black clubs and spades. Framed posters of headlining shows and entertainers lined the walls. Towering behind the sofa was a nearly life-sized vase of a white tiger. Its jug handles featured the miniature figures of Siegfried and Roy.

The red Lucite clock in Laverne's kitchen sported actual white dice to mark the hours, each rolled to the correct number. Two die were used for numbers higher than six. An inscription on the clock read: "In Vegas, It's Always Pair-a-Dice." But the real show stopper was a huge picture hanging over the kitchen table. In it, Elvis himself was crooning away at a beautiful redhead in a glittery, feathery showgirl outfit. I did a double-take.

"Is that *you*, Laverne?"

Laverne handed me a blue, turban-shaped cup filched from the Aladdin.

"Yeah, that's me, doll. Used to be, anyway."

"What happened? I mean...why did you leave Vegas?"

"Nobody lasts forever in Vegas, honey. My time was up. It was either leave as a glamour girl or stay and work the buffet 'til I dropped dead of fallen arches. Speaking of dead, you look like death warmed over, sugar. What's up?"

I took a sip of coffee.

"Man, that's good coffee, Laverne!"

"Learned from the best. Frankie taught me how."

"Frankie as in Frank Sinatra?!"

"I didn't get to live this long by telling secrets. I know when to keep my mouth shut. So spill it, gal. You're safe with me."

I blew out a breath. *What the hell.*

"I've been accused of murder and of cutting off someone's finger. And I just found out Tom's cheating on me."

"Dang, child! You want some Kahlua in that coffee?"

"If I thought it would help, I'd drink the whole bottle."

"Ah, sugar. I've lived through worse and I'm still standing. Life has a way of working things out."

"You really think so?"

"Sure. Who's the stiff?"

"Huh?"

"The guy they say you murdered."

"I don't know."

"Any way to find out?"

"Not that I can think of. Wait. I do know a guy who works in the morgue."

"Good. Call him. Now, who's this finger guy?"

"A guitar player. He's missing an eye and a tooth, too."

Laverne looked at me sideways.

"*I* didn't take them."

"You talking about Mickie?"

"What?! Yes. You *know* him?"

"Sugar, when you're as old as me, you know just about everybody. I've seen him playing gigs around town. Why on earth does Mickie think you took his finger?"

"Long story short, because I had it. I gave it to the police."

"Hmmm. Well there you go, honey."

"What?"

"Possession is nine-tenths of the law. Everybody knows that."

I'D JUST GOTTEN BACK from Laverne's house when the phone rang.

"Is this Valiant Fremden?"

Crap. "Yes."

"Ahem. I'm Ferrol Finkerman. I'm calling..."

"Look, whatever you're selling, I'm not in the mood."

"Ms. Fremden, this is serious business. I'm calling on behalf of my client, Harden Michaels. He's named you as the responsible party in a personal injury case."

"I don't know anyone named Harden Michaels."

"Oh. You might know him by his...um...*street* name. Hard-on? Mickie the Guitar Man?"

"What!?"

"Yes," Finkerman said. "My client identified you as the assailant who removed his finger by, shall we say, *force*. At any rate, he's suing you for personal injury, mental anguish and loss of lifetime career earnings."

"You've got to be kidding me. How much does he—do *you*—want?"

"How much have you got? Tell me and I'll settle for half. Don't tell me and we'll go for the whole enchilada."

"You're a total piece of dog crap, you know that?"

"Hey, with a name like Ferrol Finkerman, I was doomed. Save your insults for your husband. So, what's it gonna be, your money or your life behind bars? If we settle out of court, there's no need to get the cops involved. Mr. Michaels will drop any and all criminal charges for the right price."

What the hell! What was going on here? I needed time to think.

"Mr. Finkerman, can you give me a week to sort this out? I'll prove to you that you have the wrong person."

"I don't think so."

"Why?"

"Because you called me Mr. Finkerman. You're trying to butter me up."

"No. It's not that..."

"Listen. You had the finger, right?"

"Uh...yes."

"I'll give you two days. And some advice on the house. It doesn't look good for you. Possession is nine-tenths of the law, you know."

I CALLED LAVERNE AS soon as I got off the phone.

"Ferrol Finkerman? That guy is the biggest shyster outside The Strip."

"Why would he sue *me*?"

"Honey, you don't go digging for gold in a dumpster."

Crap! "I've gotta go, Laverne. I've got some errands to run."

"Honey, as long as you're out and about, could you give me a ride to my nail salon? I broke a nail and I can't drive."

"You can't drive because you broke a nail?"

"No, silly! I broke a nail trying to fix my car. You know anybody handy with old engines?"

"Yes, I think I do."

Chapter Twenty-One

"Get in, Laverne. Where's the nail salon?"

Laverne opened the passenger door and plopped her skinny butt on the bucket seat, her back toward me. As she twisted her torso to face forward, she folded her long legs and carefully swung them around. Her knobby knees bumped against the glovebox. Dressed in a gold velour workout suit and a million gold chains, she looked like a hip-hop grasshopper from outer space.

"What's with the grand entrance?" I asked.

"Huh?"

"The legs."

"Oh. Habit. These gams were my money-maker back in the day. One cut or bruise and I'd be off the cast until it healed. One bad scar and a girl's career could go down the drain faster than a bottle of cheap wine."

"Wow. I had no idea."

I turned the ignition. "So, where's the salon?"

"Over off of 22nd and 34th."

"Okay. Pops' place is right around the corner from there."

I cruised out of the driveway and headed toward Gulf Boulevard.

"Pops' place?"

"Oh. Earl Popkins. Pops for short. He's the old man I bought Maggie from when I was broke last year. I gave him $125 down and a handshake to pay another hundred every month until I paid Maggie off or he died, whichever came first.

Laverne shot me a dubious look.

"That's pretty harsh, honey."

"Hey! It was *his* idea, not mine. So far I've been sticking to the deal, more or less. But today Mr. Methuselah's gonna hit pay-dirt. I've got the rest of his cash in my back pocket."

"Miss Big Bucks." Laverne winked at me. "Bet he never thought he'd live to see the day."

I shrugged and grinned.

"Neither did I."

"So who's this guy Winky? The one you said could fix my car?"

"Just a guy I met at the beach last year. He fixed the air conditioning at my house last week."

"Oh. Did he get you one for a house instead of a train?"

"Uh...yes. That's what he did all right."

"Good. I wish that company would quit ripping people off."

"Right. Me too. We'll stop by Water Loo's on the way and see if Winky's there."

"Should you call him first?"

"He doesn't have a phone. But he should be there. Or his girlfriend, Winnie, will be. She'll know how to reach him."

I pulled out of Bahia Shores and chugged along Gulf Boulevard past 107th. The sky was blue and the air was still April fresh. It was good to get in a top-down cruise while the fair weather lasted. I pulled into Water Loo's parking lot and hit the brakes.

"Fair warning, Laverne. This place is a dump."

She shot me a wry grin.

"I lived in Vegas, remember?"

I opened the door and took a look inside. Water Loo's was deserted except for the corner booth. Loo and a guy I'd never seen before were having a discussion that faded away to cautious stares when Laverne and I stepped inside.

"Hi. I'm looking for Winky?" I asked.

"Who the hell's Winky?" the stranger asked.

Loo started to say something, but the man kicked him in the shin. The man sitting with Loo sported a headful of thick, grey hair styled in an Elvis pompadour. He also had the King's lips and his famous sneer.

"What?" Loo asked the guy, then turned to me. "He ain't here."

"Okay, thanks," I said. "I guess I'll be going, then."

I turned and saw Winnie coming out of the kitchen with a fresh pot of coffee.

"Hi, Val!"

"Hi Winnie. Looking for Winky. Do you know how I can get a hold of him?"

"Not really. He ain't got a phone. But he usually shows up here at the end of my shift. Around three?"

"Okay. Here's my number. Have him give me a call?"

"Sure. Who's your friend?"

"Oh. This is Laverne. She needs some car rep—"

"Hey kid with the coffee! Get your butt over here," yelled the man sitting next to Loo.

"Who's that?" I asked.

Winnie shrugged, rolled her eyes and shuffled off to serve the coffee. Laverne and I stepped out of the dingy brown hovel and into the glaring sunlight.

"What a jerk that guy was," I said.

"Yeah. He reminds me of some dirt-bag back in Vegas. What was his name? Buffalo Bill?"

"Buffalo Buffoon?" I suggested.

Laverne laughed.

"Yeah. That could be it."

LAVERNE AND I TOOLED back down Gulf and hung a left on 107th. We crossed the bridge spanning the Intracoastal and skirted through the tiny community of Treasure Island. A few blocks later we were on the mainland. We passed by Ming-Ming's on our way to 34th street.

"There's the scene of the crime." I nodded toward the restaurant as we drove by. "That's where I saw Tom and Milly together."

"You know, back in Vegas, at the casino buffets I tried every food under the sun. I never could warm up to sushi."

"Yeah. I'm starting to lose my appetite for it as well."

"Now don't you go and do that."

"Do what?"

"Let a man spoil something for you. Honey, if *I* did that, I'd be down to drive-through donuts and coffee."

"But Laverne, how do you separate the two? I mean, Ming-Ming's was *our* place."

"You know for sure he's cheating?"

"No. But come on. Milly's gorgeous. So is Tom. They'd make the perfect pair."

"There's a lot of beauty in imperfection, sugar. It makes you real. Bing told me that."

"Bing Cr...? Never mind. What's the address of the salon?"

"Uh...let's see."

Laverne fumbled around in her purse and finally pulled out a card. I hung a left onto 34th Street.

"Card says it's 2330 34th Street. Why?"

"Well, odd numbers are on one side of the road, even on the other."

"Oh. I never knew that. But zero. It's not even *or* odd, is it?"

I started to answer, then my face went slack.

"I never thought about it. I guess you're right, Laverne. Let's just call it even."

"Ooops! There it is, sugar. You just passed it."

"Crap. I'll turn around."

"I'm not in any hurry, honey. Tell me, how old is this Pops guy, anyway?"

"Probably older than you. But his wife is younger."

"Just my luck."

"Still want to come along for the ride?"

"Sure."

I cruised past 22nd Avenue and took a right. A few blocks down, I took another right. A neighborhood of small, run-down 1950s block houses just like mine came into view. But, as Florida realtors were fond of saying, "location, location, location." Without the waterfront venue, the value of these homes was about a tenth of what mine was worth.

It was one of those neighborhoods where nobody minded a couple of extra vehicles parked up in the yard. Concrete blocks instead of tires were also acceptable, and once the weeds had half-covered them, abandoned appliances were considered garden sculptures. Despite the obvious signs of neglect, the little community tugged at my heartstrings. It reminded me of my mom's place up in Greenville—minus the bass boats, ATVs and chickens running loose.

I pulled up on the street in front of Pops' house. Painted seafoam green with teal trim, it was easy to spot. Pops was out in the yard polishing the chrome on a 1970s-era gold-colored Cadillac. His black arms glistened in the sun, and looked surprisingly muscular for a man pushing eighty. If his hair hadn't been pure white, I'd have placed him in his late fifties.

"Well now, there she is!"

Pops waved his dirty polish rag at me.

"How's the old girl running?"

"Not bad, thanks for asking," Laverne yelled across my lap.

"Ha ha! Who's the looker with you, Val?"

"Laverne. Straight from Vegas," I answered.

"Well, is she now?"

Pop stood back, put a finger to his chin and stared at Laverne. I climbed out of the car.

"I've come to pay you off, Pops."

He didn't hear me. His eyes were fixed on the strawberry blonde. I took $475 out of my back pocket and waved it in his face. That got his attention.

"I said I've come to pay Maggie off, Pops. Here's the rest of what I owe you. Thanks for trusting me to pay her off in installments."

Pops counted the money, one eye on the bills, the other on Laverne. "It's all here. We're square. But wait, have twenty back."

Pops stuck a twenty in my hand.

"What? Why?"

"You just won me a bet with my wife. Worth every penny for the braggin' rights. I was right about you. Now I get to wag it in her face."

"What? I don't get it."

"Velda said you'd never pay me back. She don't trust people like I do. See, I got an eye for knowing who I can lend to and who I can't. Take this Caddy, here. This woman came by the other day. Wants that Caddy real bad. But I wouldn't let her have it without a flat thousand dollars down. The woman gave me five hundred and said she'd be back the next day with the rest. She never did do it. I knowed something wasn't right about that crazy-eyed woman."

"I guess you win some and you lose some, Pops."

"Yep. Shore enough."

Pops eyed Laverne longingly, then turned toward me and put a hand on my shoulder.

"Oh, speaking of losing, Val, sorry about your piggybank. I hope you got it back in one piece."

"What? That was *you*? You took it?"

"Well, yes and no. I knew about it, but it was Velda's doings. We was driving by one day, and saw little Maggie parked at the drugstore. You were a day or so late with a payment. My wife made me pull over. She wanted me to go inside the store and shake you down for the money. But I wouldn't do it. Well, she got mad and swiped that piggybank instead. As collateral, mind you. She didn't trust you like I did. Velda thought that little peanut bank was full of the money you wasn't paying us. But when she opened the bottom, wasn't nothing but dust inside. I carried that bank around with me for months, trying to see if I could get it back to you. I finally did a couple weeks ago."

"'Sorry, Mr. P.' That was you."

"Yep. Hope it wasn't no inconvenience."

Nope. Just made Glad miss her own funeral. "No worries."

"Good. Now don't go blaming Velda. We've got cheated a few times. In this business, it happens. Like that crazy woman wantin' this Cadillac. She called me a week ago, trying to get her deposit back. Said some guy called Bingo was gonna get her. You ever hear such nonsense? She was a looney bird. I hadn't seen hide nor hair of her since."

"Bingo! That's it!" Laverne said.

"That's what?" I asked.

"Bingo Bob. That's the name of that jerk at Water Loo's."

Chapter Twenty-Two

"Who's Bingo Bob?" I asked Laverne as I hit the gas and waved goodbye to Pops.

"Just some low-life who ran one of the bingo games at the Gold Digger Casino back in Vegas. I heard he was a bookie for sports games, too. But that was what...fifteen years ago? I wonder how he ended up here in Florida."

"Same as everyone. People come here from all over. They think Florida's the secret to the good life. No snow. Just fun in the sun all year long. That, and they can live in their cars through the winter and not freeze to death. Everybody blames Florida for being loaded with crazy people, but I swear Laverne, most of them come here from somewhere else."

Laverne looked at me through the top of her sunglasses.

"Sugar, nobody looks good in jade."

I blew out a breath. "Sorry, Laverne. I've just...I've got a load of stuff going on right now. I've got to figure out what the hell's going on with that blasted finger. I can't get sued back down to nothing. Not again."

"Well, what are you working with? What have you got so far?"

"Not much. I found the finger in the couch that day you came over for coffee."

"The day you beat the stuffing out of those pillows in your back-yard?"

"Yeah."

"That's the same day I fixed your faucet."

"Yep. That's the day."

"Well, who could have put a finger in your couch to begin with?"

"That's just it. Tom brought the couch over. It had been sitting in the alley behind my old apartment all day. I talked to the bum who'd been sleeping on it. He told me the finger belonged to that guy Mickie. You know. The one with the eye patch and gold tooth."

"Yeah. So, Mickie ought to know how he lost his own finger."

"Yes, he ought to. But he says *I* cut it off. And now he's suing me."

"What? That's crazy. How is that possible?"

"He says he was drunk at the time. He couldn't see me because I put a sack over his head. But he recognized my *voice*."

I pulled up in front of the nail salon. Laverne climbed out.

"We'll get to the bottom of this, sugar. Don't you worry."

"Thanks. Pick you up in half an hour?"

"Sounds about right."

I hit the gas and drove about thirty feet when the phone rang. It was Tom. I pulled into a parking spot.

"Yeah?"

"Val? Is everything all right?"

"Not really."

"What's going on?"

That's what I'd like to know, you cheating, lying, philandering dirt bag! "Nothing much. Just got threatened with a lawsuit by that slimy ambulance chaser Ferrol Finkerman."

"What? For what?"

"His client is missing a finger and swears I'm the one who cut it off."

"Crap, Val!"

"Yep. Crap describes the situation, all right. Deep crap."

"I don't know if I should even mention this now. You seem upset."

"Mention what?" *That you're dumping me for Milly?*

"I was going to ask you to this police benefit thing tomorrow night. But I guess you're not interested."

"What's the benefit?"

"Exactly."

"No, I mean, what's the event?"

"A dance at the old Coliseum. They're raising money for charity."

"How long have you known about it?"

"A month."

"Oh."

"You know I hate to dance."

"So what changed your mind?" *Guilty conscience?*

"My boss sort of made it clear today that my attendance was mandatory."

"So you're stuck having to go, and thought of me. How sweet."

"Look. If you don't want to go—"

"Oh, no. I want to go. Sounds delightful. What time?"

"Pick you up at seven?"

"Sounds perfect."

I clicked off the phone. *Well, Mr. Tom Foreman, you're about to find out exactly what you're gonna be missing. I'll be smoking hot at that dance. You and Milly Halbert can eat your hearts out and kiss my behind! Once you see how fantastic I really am, I'm going to dump you both like a pair of day-old dirty diapers.*

I pulled Maggie into a parking spot, scrambled out of the car and marched over to the nail salon. The young Asian woman at the reception desk looked up from filing her nails.

"How much for a manicure?"

The girl looked at my hands.

"Lady, we Beauty Nail. Not Miracle Nail."

"SHOW ME THOSE CAT CLAWS again!"

Laverne and I were cruising down Central Avenue, heading toward Pasadena Boulevard. I let go of the wheel and pawed the air with my long, shiny, bright-red nails.

"Ha ha! Good to see some sass back in you, sugar! Now let's find a dress that matches that attitude."

I pulled up in front of my favorite shop on Corey Avenue. The window display was full of pastel-colored sundresses and cute beach wear. Laverne turned her nose up.

"Sugar, this is amateur-hour stuff. Start the car. I know just the place with the ammunition you need to bring down the big game."

I swung the car around and headed back toward Central Avenue and downtown.

"You can't catch someone's attention with the same-old-same-old, girl. You've got to kick it up a notch. Take him by surprise."

"You mean like he did me—with Milly?"

"Nope. Better than that."

Laverne pointed to her right.

"Slow down. Just another block on the right. See it?"

I did. It was a consignment store. I blew out a disappointed sigh.

"Laverne, that place is full of junk."

"Yes, it most certainly is. One man's junk is another man's treasure. That's what you're after, right? Make him realize what a treasure he's letting go of?"

"Yes...."

"All right then. Let's go."

Chapter Twenty-Three

"Here, honey. Stick these in there."

Between her thumbs and index fingers, Laverne dangled two globs of rubber that looked like oversized, raw chicken breasts.

"What in the world *are* they?" I asked.

"They're chicken fill-its. At least that's what the girls from England called 'em back in the day. Saved many a flat-chested girl's career."

I stared at the strange, floppy globs.

"Oh, don't be shy, honey!"

Laverne reached a boney, red-nailed hand into my dress and slipped a cold, slimy glob under my right breast. She jiggled it around until it filled out the right side of my dress's bodice perfectly. I looked in the mirror and was instantly converted.

"Whoa! Gimme the other one!"

Laverne grinned. I grabbed the other fill-it from her hand and in-stalled it myself. I stared at my reflection and shimmied my shoulders. I was rocking it!

"*Jessica Rabbit*, eat my dust!"

"*Now* you're talking, sugar!"

In under ten minutes and for less than twenty bucks, Laverne had transformed me into a Vegas showgirl, minus the giant feather head-dress. Amongst the castoffs in that old consignment store that smelled of desperation and soured dreams, she'd scrounged around and found a vintage, backless, red-sequin dress that fit me like a wet glove. It clung to my body like a desperate lover—everywhere except the boob area, that is. Laverne had solved that problem with a pair of falsies.

"You want the whole vamp treatment?" Laverne asked.

I was feeling cheeky.

"Sure. Why not."

Laverne fiddled with my hair. Armed with nothing but a comb and a half a can of Aqua Net, she puffed and curled my hair until it was twice its normal size. Satisfied, she swirled my long bangs over one eye like a sexy pinup model and hosed them down with hairspray.

"Just a touch of red lipstick and we're done here," she said.

She handed me the lipstick and pinched me on the butt. I jerked back and scowled at her.

"Ouch! What was that for?"

"For good luck, sugar. But you're not gonna need it. You're a knockout!"

I looked in the mirror again. Yes. I *was* a knockout. And I knew just who I was aiming to punch in the gut.

I TALKED A BIG GAME, but when it came to follow through, I'd proven time and again that my bark was bigger than my bite. I poured myself a TNT to steady my nerves. I was taking my first sip when the phone rang and nearly startled me out of my silver stilettos.

"Hello?"

"Hey, Val. It's Milly. What are you up to tonight?"

Wouldn't you like to know. Or do you already? Did I say "yes" to Tom and spoil your plans? "Going out with Tom. You?"

"Oh. Nothing. Just wanted to see if you could come out and play."

"Not tonight."

"What are you two doing?"

"Why?"

"No reason, Val. Just curious."

"Nothing special. Look, I've got to go. I see Tom driving up."

"Okay, have fun."

"Thanks. I'm *planning* on it."

I clicked off the phone just as Tom rang the bell. I straightened my dress, ran a finger along my stiff bangs and flung open the door. Tom's usual boyish grin evaporated. His eyes grew as big as poached eggs.

"Whoa! Val? Is that *you* under all that?"

"Yes."

"You look...you...I...I can't take you to the charity benefit looking like that!"

"What? Why not?" *You jerk-wad!*

"You look way too sexy for that place. You should be at...a fancy hotel in Vegas or something."

"Are you saying I look trampy?"

"What? No. Just a bit...*fancy*...for the occasion, I mean."

"Then go on without me."

I pushed the door to close it. Tom raised a hand and held it open.

"Wait a minute! What's up? I didn't mean to hurt your feelings."

"That's what they all say."

"Come on, Val. You look great. I'm sorry. Let's go."

TOM WENT TO FETCH ME a gin and tonic. I looked around the inside of the Coliseum. It was built back when dancing was what couples did on a Friday night. The building was pretty much a huge, rectangular, wooden dance floor with a roof overhead for good measure. Along two sides, intimate little booths were niched into the stucco walls. The thirty-foot ceiling was rounded like an airport hangar. Chandeliers hung from it like diamond pendants. A six-piece band in tuxedoes were busy setting up on the stage at the opposite end.

I felt right at home in my sparkly vintage outfit. I imagined myself back in the 1930s. A femme fatale in a too-tight red dress. All I was missing was a vial of poison tucked between my boobs. I'd have to settle for sweat.

"Here's your TNT, miss dynamite."

I spun around and almost lost my balance. I looked up at Tom. *Dang it.* Just like my daydream, he was too good to be true. Tom would look handsome in a wheelbarrow full of cow manure. Put him in a charcoal suit with a red tie, and it just wasn't fair. A girl didn't have a chance.

Tom slid his warm hand along the small of my naked back. Traitorous lust shot through me like an injection of liquid fire.

"Should we find a seat?" he asked.

"Sure," I said, hoping my dress wouldn't split in half when I sat down.

Tom led me to a table near the stage that had been reserved for police officers. When we walked up, half the guys' eyes bulged out of their heads. I grinned smugly. A balding man in his mid-forties took off his glasses and eyed me up and down.

"Tom. You lucky dog! She makes the rest of our wives look like chopped liv—"

The woman sitting next to the bald guy elbowed him in the ribs. His glasses flew back to his nose and he hunkered down to grovel with his angry, glaring wife. Tom touched my back again, and pulled a chair out for me. I lowered myself slowly, hoping the material would hold. It did. Tom sat next to me, squeezed my hand and whispered in my ear.

"He's right, you know. You're the most gorgeous woman in the room."

I didn't want to like his words, but I did anyway. "Thanks."

The band started up, and began to play one of my favorites, *Just the Way You Look Tonight.* I couldn't resist.

"Dance with me," I whispered in Tom's ear.

He whispered back. "I promise. In bed tonight."

I pulled back as if he'd spit in my ear.

"No. *Now*. Come on. It's my favorite song."

"Okay, okay. But I'm not guaranteeing the safety of your toes."

"I'll take the chance."

I yanked Tom toward the dance floor. It was filling up fast with middle-aged couples dancing cheek-to-cheek. Tom pulled me to his chest and began to sway. The soft lighting, the feel of him close to me, it should have been magical. But every time I drifted off into a dream that things would be all right between us, a finger poked me awake and reminded me of Mickie and Ming Ming's and Milly. Oh my.

The music stopped abruptly. Someone spoke over the microphone. The dancing couples came to a standstill.

"Just a couple of quick announcements, folks! Hope you are enjoying the music of Sandy Flats!"

The man speaking onstage was swimming around in an ill-fitting tuxedo. His expression was that of a self-congratulatory, overblown prick. Either that, or my attitude about men in general was in desperate need of adjusting. It was a tough call.

"That's Jergen's dear old dad," Tom whispered.

I looked again. Nope. I was right the first time. That man was as smug as my cousin Tammy Jeeter at our family reunions.

"Hello everyone. I'm Chief of Police Franz Jergen. I just wanted to thank everyone for turning out to the benefit. You all look mighty fancy! Some more than others! Ha ha! I just wanted to take a minute to give a special thanks to Officer Hans Jergen for setting up the benefit. Oh. Excuse me. I meant to say, *Lieutenant* Hans Jergen. Congratulations on the promotion, Lieutenant Jergen!"

A round of applause broke out, but the smiles on the policemen's faces seemed forced. As the music started up again, Tom leaned in close and whispered in my ear.

"No surprise there. He's been on the force *three* freaking years. Me? *Twenty!* Now we're on the same level. Jerks. Both of them."

So this *was the bad blood between Tom and Hans Jergen? Is that why he wouldn't come to the house when he knew Jergen was going to be there? Was Tom's pride more important to him than my safety?*

The band started up again with *Jack the Knife.*

"Let's go sit down," Tom said.

"Oh no, mister. I've come here to dance, and we're going to dance."

"I'm not in the mood."

I grabbed Tom's hand and put it on my waist. *You hate to dance? Too bad!*

"Come on, don't be a jerk, Tom. Show me what you've got."

"You really do have to have it your way, don't you?"

Before I could answer, Tom grabbed my hand and twirled me around. He yanked me in close to him, but his eyes seemed bitter and distant. He spun me out hard, then pulled me back again with such force that I bumped into his chest. He faltered. His shoe came down hard on my silver stiletto. I tripped and lunged sideways.

Just before my face hit the floor, Tom caught me by the ribs and hauled me up in a vertical Heimlich maneuver. I gasped, and one of my chicken fill-its flew the coop. I watched in slow-motion horror as it bounced like a ball of peach Jell-O across the wooden floor. The sole of a shiny black loafer squashed down on it, and a man fell hard, face-first at my feet.

He scrambled up in a huff and picked up the rubber boob.

"Who's is this?" he demanded.

The man was Lieutenant Hans Jergen. *Oh, crap!*

The crowd came to a standstill. They gathered in a circle around us like schoolkids waiting for a fight to break out. I tried to look innocent, but as peoples' eyes scanned the group, they invariably settled on me. It was impossible not to notice my dress's crumpled right bodice. Compared to the left side, it looked like a deflated air bag. Jergen's eyes found my chest, then my face.

"*You* again!"

"I...I...uh...."

I looked over at Tom. He was livid, but holding it in. Jergen turned his wrath on Tom.

"Lieutenant Foreman. Perfect. It figures. You two are of the same *caliber.*"

"What's that supposed to mean?" I asked.

Jergen whipped his head around to face me.

"You're a *criminal.* And so is *he.*"

"What?"

I followed Jergen's eyes over to Tom. He stood there motionless, arms folded, and didn't say a word. *What a coward!*

"Ms. Fremden, correct?" Jergen said, his voice full of disdain.

I stared at the floor. "Yes."

"I've got a suspicious body in the morgue with your name on it. And today I took a statement from a man charging you with cutting off his finger. If I hadn't been so busy with the benefit today, I'd have already paid you a visit and read you your rights."

My gut went limp. Jergen turned to Tom.

"And you. She probably doesn't even know about your unspeakable crime."

Jergen looked back at me, his face twisted with anger and disgust.

"Or did he happen to mention that he got my sister pregnant and left her in the lurch?"

"What?!"

I grabbed the falsie from Officer Jergen's hand and spat at both men with my eyes.

"How could you, Tom? I'm leaving! Don't follow me!"

Tom took a step toward me.

"Val, wait!"

I turned and glared at the crowd like a psychotic cow.

"What are you people looking at?" I screeched. "Show's over!"

The bystanders parted like the Red Sea to let me pass. I stuffed the chicken fill-it back in my dress and stomped toward the exit. Despite my demand for him not to, Tom followed behind. When I got outside, he grabbed my shoulder and spun me around.

"Where are you going, Val?"

"Home!"

"You're not even going to let me explain?"

"What's to explain, Tom? I get it. I know everything about you that I care to know. It's over. I'm taking a cab home. Don't bother calling me again. *Ever!*"

Chapter Twenty-Four

I couldn't see. The left side of my face was crushed into the pillow. I blinked again, but my right eye's vision remained fuzzy and black. *Had I finally drunk myself blind?*

I reached up to touch my face. My fingertips landed on the stiff hide of a dead animal.

"Aaahhh!"

I shot up in bed. The horrid beast came with me. I tried to yank it off my head, but it held on tight like a superglued weasel. I freaked and scrambled out of bed, screaming like a raving lunatic. I ran to the bathroom. One look in the mirror made my gut go limp and my hands fall to my sides. The beastly creature on top of my head was the rigid, repellant remains of last-night's spray-lacquered hairdo.

I scrounged around for a barrette and pinned back the stiff bangs hovering over my right eye like a coconut husk. My once nicely made-up face looked like a Picasso reject. And I was still wearing that trashy, thrift-store dress. Laverne had hooked and zipped me into it yesterday. Last night, I'd wrestled around with it until I'd nearly dislocated my shoulder, but I couldn't get it off. I'd slept in the sequined straightjacket with nothing for company but a broken heart and a bottle of gin.

I stumbled back to the bedroom and tripped over a wayward blob of rubber on the floor. When I leaned over to pick up the falsie, the backside of the dress ripped clear to my waist. *Nice.* I padded to the kitchen for a pair of scissors and cut the halter-neck off me like a used-

137

up flea collar, then twisted the dress around on my hips until I could reach the hooks. I undid them, zipped the dress down to my thigh and let it fall to the floor. I stepped out of it and stared at the red-sequin puddle at my feet. It glistened on the tile like the bloody remains of my dead relationship with Tom.

Even with your life at stake, you made impressing a man your number-one priority. Great job, Val. It was so worth it.

STEAMY WATER, A LOOFAH and a bottle of shampoo went to work on my face and hair until no traces of last night's fiasco remained. I stepped out of the shower, toweled off, pulled on my bathrobe and padded to the kitchen to fix myself a cappuccino. I sipped it and googled the news. As far as I could tell, there were no reports about a dead man in a dumpster, me getting charged with cutting off Mickie's finger, or the police benefit turning into a roadhouse brawl.

Well, at least I could take consolation in the fact that nobody else knew about my life going to hell in a handbasket.

I lay back in bed, let the caffeine kick in and tried to remember the last time I'd gone to Sunset Beach. It must have been more than a month ago. I was way overdue for some fresh salt air and sunshine. Maybe it would clear my head. It wouldn't hurt to see the guys, either. I could really use some friends right now.

It was nearly 9 a.m. when I threw my straw tote onto Maggie's passenger seat. The sky was clear and the sun was already beating down strong enough to make the fake-leather seats toasty-warm to the touch. I slapped a floppy hat on my head and turned the ignition. The engine's roar reminded me that I needed to talk to Winky about Laverne's car. I couldn't remember whether I'd already talked to him about fixing it or not. With all the crazy stuff that had been going on, my mind had become way too squirrely to trust.

Maggie rumbled out of the driveway and I steered her toward Gulf Boulevard. I hung a left and headed south to Sunset Beach, the home of Glad's beloved beach bar, Caddy's. It was Sunday, so I was pretty sure Winky, Jorge and Goober would be there. Under Florida law, no one could sell booze before 11 a.m. The guys usually idled away the once-a-week dry spell at one of Caddy's picnic tables in the sand. If I got there early enough, they'd still be sober.

The radio was playing *All I Need is a Miracle* by Mike & The Mechanics. *How apropos.* I smiled wryly, then turned up the volume and sang along.

"*I knew you were never right...I'll admit I was never wrong...*"

A DJ's voice broke over the radio, cutting off the song.

"Jack Hammer here! It's nine o'clock, friends and fiends! You know what that means. It's time to get down and dirty with the latest edition of *Blurs & Slurs*. You don't want to miss this one, folks. It's a classic! Let's get to it!"

A very, very, very drunk woman's voice cracked over the radio.

"Jack...I had...I had just like...a big (BLEEP) blowout with my boyfriend. Oops. I mean...ex boyfriend."

"Really now, darling. What started it?"

"The chicken thingy...it fell out of my boob."

The world around me came to a quiet standstill. My mind erased itself. I could see the train wreck ahead, but I couldn't stop it. I was the drunk engineer at the wheel. My mouth sagged open. The rest of me was mortified to paralysis.

"Yes," the D.J. egged on. "I hate when that happens."

"Right? You understand...don't you Jack?"

"Yes, I sure do. Then what happened?"

"He had...he had a lady with a baby."

"That must have been...painful."

"Yeshh! And that's...not half of it."

"No? Please, tell me the other half!"

"He gave me a (BLEEP) couch for my birthday...and then the dwarf came to get me."

"Your boyfriend's a dwarf?"

"No. He's a cheater. A cheating (BLEEP)!"

"How do you know?"

"I didn't...tell you? He ate...he ate...my girlfriend's...sushi."

"Naughty boy."

"Yeshh! It's his fault...'cause of the finger."

"The finger? Sounds like you got the finger from your boyfriend."

"No! I got the finger...from the *couch*. And now...now the cops are after me."

"You certainly have an interesting life. What's your name?"

"Val Shremshend."

"Well, thanks for calling in Val. Anything more to add?"

"I think I just farted...."

"Ha ha ha! People! Didn't I tell you? A classic! We'll be playing this one for weeks. You just can't make this (BLEEP) up!"

A horn honked behind me. I was idling at a green light. I hit the gas and turned right. *Where was I going? What was I doing?* I drove by a strange man. He was laughing. Was he laughing at *me?*

My phone rang. It was Tom. I cringed and looked away. The sign for Caddy's caught my eye. I pulled into the parking lot and turned off Maggie's ignition. I sunk my head on the steering wheel and decided then and there to swear off booze and men forever.

"HEY, IS THAT THE INFAMOUS Val Shremshend?" Goober called to me from a picnic table on the beach behind Caddy's.

Oh crap! I ducked my head in shame. I wanted to hide under a rock. I wanted to drown in the ocean. I wanted to make a clean getaway and start a new life in another country. *Oh yeah. I tried that already. It didn't work.* I turned the ignition on Maggie, but Jorge and Winky walked up behind her and blocked my escape.

"Welcome to the *Blurs & Slurs Club*, Val," Winky teased. "'Bout time, I'd say. What's this I hear about a chicken in your boob?"

"Arrrgh!"

Winky patted my shoulder with a freckled hand.

"Ha ha, don't take it so bad, Val. We all been there."

I looked up from the steering wheel.

"On *Blurs & Slurs*?"

"Yep."

"Even you, Jorge?"

Jorge shrugged guiltily.

"Jes. A long time ago."

I sunk back in my seat and put a hand over my eyes.

"How long does it take for the pain and humiliation to go away?"

"What pain and humiliation?" Winky asked. "You're a freakin' movie star now! Soon as it hits 'leven, I'm buying you a beer!"

I peeked at Winky from between my fingers and did a double take. He actually seemed to be genuinely *proud* of me! My hand dropped and my back straightened.

"Thanks, Winky. But I think I just decided to give up drinking."

"What? Now *that's* some crazy talk."

I snickered despite myself. "Winky, you don't have the money to buy me a beer."

"I shore do. Look!"

Winky pulled a worn, plastic wallet from his cargo shorts and pulled out three crisp twenty-dollar bills.

"Woah! Where'd you get that kind of money?"

"You should know. I been working last couple a days fixin' a guy's air conditioner, just like I did at your place."

"Why should I know that?"

"Well, you got me back in the fixin' mood. I hadn't touched a motor in years. After fixin' that AC for you, I started tellin' folks about it, and pickin' up a bit a work here and there."

"Good for you."

"Yep. One feller was kinda persnickety. He wanted a reference. I give him your name and number. He called back an hour later and hired me on the spot."

"Really?"

"Yep. Feels good to have my hands under the hood again. Thanks for telling him I did a bang-up job."

"Winky, I never told anyone that. He never called me."

"Huh. Well, maybe I give him the wrong number. Anyway, he knowed by my honest face that I was a hard-working man."

"You're kidding, right?"

Winky's proud smile faded a notch.

"Didn't yore momma teach you to play nice?"

"Sorry, Winky. You're right. How's this for nice? Would you like to help Laverne fix her engine?"

"Now come on, Val. You know I already got my hands full with Winnie."

Chapter Twenty-Five

I'd hung my head in shame and braced for a heap of humiliation from the guys about my *Blurs & Slurs* debut. But they'd surprised me. My dialing disaster had had the exact opposite effect. It had actually earned me street credit. I'd passed an unspoken rite of derelict passage; I'd committed and survived an act of complete and utter public humiliation.

At the picnic table, Winky had bought me that beer to celebrate. I'd drunk it gratefully, and listened to Goober as he'd lain out the story of his own grisly turn at bat, right after his divorce five years ago. Before I left, we'd toasted Glad, and a feeling akin to camaraderie had crept into my heart as our voices rang out together, chanting my mom's signature salutation: "Screw you, kiddo!"

Maggie's seats had been almost at lava level when I'd skootched into the driver's seat at 2 p.m. I'd checked my phone to find Tom had called four times. The fifth time he'd left a text. It read, "Please. Let me explain. It's complicated."

With men, it seemed, it always was.

I WENT HOME AND GOOGLED the news again. Still nothing. Not even about *Blurs & Slurs*. I sighed with relief. It lasted about a minute. Then my phone rang.

"Hello?"

"Valiant Fremden?"

"Uh...yes."

"Offi...*Lieutenant* Jergen here."

I braced for another kind of impact. Was he calling to tell me I'm under arrest? I took Winky's advice. I played nice.

"Yes. Congratulations, lieutenant. What can I do for you?"

My graciousness must have caught him off guard. His voice softened a smidge.

"Oh. Well, thank you. I'm calling to let you know we've identified the body of the man found in the dumpster. His name is Warren Harris. Are you acquainted with this man?'

"No. I've never heard of him. Why do you think this is the guy?"

"He's missing the correct finger, and his initials match the ring in question."

"Really? W-H...couldn't that also be H-M? If you turned the ring around?"

"I suppose so. Why?"

"The man who accused me of cutting his finger off. His name is Harden Michaels."

"Yes. That's correct. How do you know that?"

"I...I'm not sure I should be speaking with you about this."

"Ms. Fremden, I'm not the bad guy here. Your philandering boyfriend is."

"He's not my boyfriend anymore."

"Well, I'm glad to hear it. The man is a menace to women in general."

"I guess you think *I'm* a menace to *men* in general."

"You said it, not me."

"Have a nice day, lieutenant."

"I will. But I can't guarantee the same for you."

"What's that supposed to mean?"

His answer to the question was to hang up the phone. My gut wadded into a knot.

Crap! What am I supposed to do now? Call the cops? I blew out a big breath. The cops weren't an option. It was time to eat crow.

I hit redial for attorney Marvin Hemingway, the lawyer Mr. Fellows had referred to me. The same one I'd blown off so casually just two days ago. I was surprised and unprepared when he answered the phone himself on the first ring.

"Hello, Hemingway here."

"Oh! Mr. Hemingway. It's...um...Val Fremden."

"Who?"

"Val Fremden. Uh...Mr. Fellows gave me—"

"Oh. Yes. The woman with the missing finger."

I winced. "Um...yes. Are you still interested in taking the case? There have been some...*developments*."

"Really? Like what?"

"A lawsuit, for starters. Have you heard of Ferrol Finkerman?"

The man's voice dropped an octave. "Unfortunately, yes."

"His client is claiming to be the man missing that finger. He's threatening to sue me for personal injury and loss of career earnings."

"Threatening? Did he offer you some kind of deal?"

"Kind of. Half my money now, or all of it in court."

"Not the worst deal I've heard. Why aren't you taking it?"

"Seriously? Because *I didn't do it.*"

"You had the finger, didn't you?"

"Yes."

"Well, you know, possession is nine tenths—"

"Look, Mr. Hemingway. I need help. I didn't do this. My boyfriend—*ex* boyfriend—brought an old couch into my house. I found a finger in it. I gave it to the cops. Some dwarf in an Alfred E. Neuman mask broke in looking for it. I kicked him in the—"

"Wait a minute," Hemingway interrupted. "Alfred E. Neuman?"

"The kid from *Mad Magazine*."

"Oh. Okay. Continue."

"Really?" I said. "You ask about the mask, but not the dwarf?"

"Believe it or not, Ms. Fremden, yours is not the strangest story I've heard. I deal with a lot of carnies from Gibsonton."

Unbelievable.

"Okay," I said. "So, this dwarf breaks in, I tell him I gave the finger to the cops and he cusses up a storm. Then he says, 'mother of macaroons,' and runs out the door."

I waited for his response. There was only silence.

"Hello?"

"I'm sorry, Ms. Fremden. I can't represent you."

I nearly swallowed my tonsils. "What? Why?"

"Let's just call it a conflict of interest."

"Wait!"

"Good day."

Hemingway clicked off the phone. The doorbell rang.

Freaking flop-wads! Now what?

I opened the door. Laverne stood there looking like a starving orange mule in a pink velour jumpsuit. She took one look at me and her smile evaporated into a scowl.

"Looks like someone's been up all night arguing with the voice of reason."

"I guess that's one way to put it."

"Did you win or lose?"

"I'd say I lost. Definitely."

"Too bad. Huh. I thought you'd be in a good mood. Revenge is supposed to be sweet, right? So, how'd it go last night?"

"Huh?"

"The party benefit thingy."

"Oh."

It seemed like it had happened a week ago.

"I really don't want to talk about it."

"Are you gonna invite me in or leave me hanging here like a door-to-door salesman?"

"Oh. Sorry. Come in. I'll go get your chicken fill-its."

"Keep 'em. I don't need 'em anymore."

"Okay, thanks. I think I might have ruined them, anyway."

"How do you ruin a glob of rubber?"

"Laverne, I really don't want to talk about it. Do you need something? I'm sorry, but I've got a lot on my plate right now. Tom and I broke up for good last night, and the attorney I thought was going to save me from Finkerman fired me before I had a chance to hire him."

"Why?"

"I don't know. I was explaining what happened to him and all of a sudden he shut up like a clam with laryngitis."

"That's strange."

"Yeah. It is. But Laverne, like I said, I'm busy. Did you need something?"

"I just wanted to know if you ever got a chance to talk to Winky about fixing my car. I can't do another Über. Some of those people are nuts."

"Oh. I'm sorry Laverne. Yes. I actually talked to him this morning. He said he could come by anytime."

"Great. Could you call him? Or his girlfriend? Let's get this thing going."

"Okay. I'll do it right now."

Laverne smiled, pleased as punch, as I tapped the screen on my cell phone. Winnie picked up on the third ring.

"Hi, Winnie? It's Val."

"Hey Val. You looking for Winky?"

"Yes. Is he there?"

"Yeah. I'll get him."

"Thanks, I really appreciate it. How are things going with you two?"

"Better than with Loo and Latrina. They've been at each other's throats all morning. Hey, that's funny."

"Fighting is funny?"

"No. I mean...if I couldn't hear Latrina yelling from the kitchen right now, I'd swear I was talking with her on the phone. I never noticed it before, but you sound just like her."

"Winnie, tell Winky to hold tight. I'll be right there."

Chapter Twenty-Six

"What's going on?" Laverne asked when I clicked off the phone.

"I don't have time to explain. You can either wait 'til later or ride with me to Water Loo's."

"Well, then, I'm riding with you, honey."

We jumped in the old Ford and made a beeline toward the restaurant.

"Is this about Winky?" Laverne asked. She clasped her hands on her boney knees, trying to keep them from knocking against Maggie's metal dashboard.

"No. Winky can wait. It's about Latrina. Winnie said I sounded like Latrina over the phone. Mickie, the guy who lost his finger? He said he heard *me* tell someone to cut his finger off. It must have been Latrina, because it sure as hell wasn't me."

"Why would this Latrina woman want to cut off Mickie's finger?"

"I don't know, Laverne. That's what we're going to find out."

I careened Maggie into the lot at Water Loo's just in time to see Loo driving away. A grey-haired guy was in the passenger seat, but I couldn't make him out.

"Laverne, any idea who that guy is in the car with Loo?"

"It could have been Bingo Bob, sugar. But I'm not a hundred percent sure."

We scrambled out of the old Ford. I trotted to the grimy entry door and flung it open like a six-shooter cowboy in a Western showdown. The place was almost empty and eerily quiet.

Without Loo around to argue with, Latrina had gone mute and disappeared. Winnie dropped a grimy washrag and looked up. She'd been busy pretending to wipe down the corner booth while Winky flirted with her. Jorge was sitting opposite Winky, his head down on the table, his fingers wrapped around an empty beer bottle.

"Hey, Val Pal!" Winky hollered across the restaurant. I gave him a nod and motioned for his girlfriend to come over to me.

"Hey Winnie. I need to talk to you a minute."

Winky slapped on a look of mock suspicion and hollered across the room.

"Hey now, Val. Don't you be gettin' any ideas. Winnie's mine. I saw her first."

"Don't worry. This is official business," I called back.

Winky twisted his lips skeptically. Laverne followed me and Winnie over to the coffee counter stacked with dirty dishes.

"Where's Latrina?" I asked Winnie.

"Weird. You know, you sound more like her over the phone than in person. Maybe it's because she's always yelling. It makes her voice higher pitched, more like yours."

"Winnie, this is important. I really need to talk to Latrina."

A furrow appeared in Winnie's pudgy forehead. Her bottom lip pooched out.

"Okay. I'll go get her for you."

Winnie disappeared behind a metal kitchen door smudged with filthy handprints. She came out a few seconds later, her head hanging like a whipped dog.

"She says she's busy. You need to make an appointment."

"Busy? What could she possibly be doing?"

I pushed past Winnie into the kitchen. What I saw inside made me want to go home and suck on a bottle of bleach. One thing was for sure. I'd never drink another cup of coffee at Water Loo's again as long as I lived.

Latrina was hunched over a table, back to me, studying a computer screen covered in tables and charts. Without my cheater glasses, I couldn't make out squat. Latrina scribbled something on a piece of paper, then used the pencil to scratch a spot underneath a raggedy bun of thick, frizzy black hair. The thought that I sounded like this shrieking shrew made my face scrunch into a self-pity frown.

"I need to talk to you," I said.

Latrina's eyes never left the computer screen.

"I told that girl to tell you to make an appointment."

"She did. Look. I know you cut off Mickie's finger."

Latrina whipped around, her eyes as black as a raven's.

"Who the hell told you that?"

I played a wild card. "Bingo Bob."

"That creep! Can't trust *nobody* anymore. Well, he's a liar. *I* didn't do it. *Loo* did. These jerks are always trying to make me take the hit for their bull crap!"

"*Loo* did it? Why did Loo cut off Mickie's finger?"

Latrina's face twisted with suspicion.

"Wait a minute...I didn't say *Loo* did it. You wasn't hearing me right."

"Really? What *did* you say, then?"

"Who the hell are you? The freaking cops?"

"No. I'm...a friend."

"Friend my foot! I seen you around. You been spying on me or something? Get the hell out of here. I don't want to see your ugly face in here again!"

Latrina picked up a knife and stabbed the air in my direction. I jumped back like I'd been shoved.

"Any more dumb-ass questions, '*friend*,' and your finger's next!"

Latrina stood up and lunged toward me. I turned tail and high-stepped it across the kitchen, pushed through the grimy door and ran headlong into Winnie. We crashed together, face-to-face, onto the floor. Landing on Winnie was like doing a belly flop onto a lumpy mattress. I rolled off of her and tried to suck some air back into my lungs.

Winnie sat up and adjusted her glasses.

"What's going on, Val?"

"Act like you don't know me," I whispered. "I'll explain later."

I scrambled to my feet. Latrina kicked open the kitchen door and screamed.

"I told you to get the hell out of here, witch. I mean *now!*"

"I'm leaving!" I shouted. "Your waitress was in the way. She wouldn't let me pass by until you said it was okay."

Latrina glanced down at Winnie. She was still on the floor, but had pushed herself up to sitting.

"Good work. Let her go."

Latrina's raven eyes locked on me.

"But if you see her in here again, let me know. We'll make some *la-dyfinger* sandwiches."

Latrina grinned and chopped the air with her knife. I backed away, then turned and scampered around the coffee counter. Winky, Jorge and Laverne were standing in a row, open-mouthed, like kids waiting for a dose of castor oil. Winky started to speak. I raised my right hand and discretely ran a slash-throat finger across my neck. All three blinked over at Latrina and stared, wide-eyed and silent. I grabbed Laverne's arm and marched us out of Water Loos like two indignant floozies.

"What the hell-fire happened in there, Val?" Laverne asked when the door closed behind us.

"I...I got what I came for. Loo did it. He...cut Mickie's finger off."

My knees nearly buckled. I hobbled over to Maggie, turned the ignition with my trembling hand, and backed out of the parking lot like someone learning to drive a stick shift. After I'd put half a mile's distance between me and Latrina, I could finally breath enough to speak normally.

"I'm so sorry for involving you in all this, Laverne."

"Are you kidding? This is the most excitement I've had since Elvis left the building."

I glanced over at her. The old woman in the pink velour suit was grinning from ear to ear.

"Thanks...for being there for me."

"My pleasure kid. What's an adventure without someone to share it with?"

"You sound like a greeting card."

"Yeah? Well, I hear there's worse things to sound like."

Laverne winked at me. I smiled despite myself and hit the gas.

THE AFTERNOON SKY THREATENED thunderstorms. The tourists that normally thronged along Gulf Boulevard were tucked safely away in their rooms watching TV or getting drunk at a hotel bar. With no pedestrians to dodge, Laverne and I made it back home in under five minutes. I pulled Maggie into the drive and hit the button for the ragtop. It squealed and moaned and whined like an electric can opener until the canvas top hung in the air about three feet above the front seats. At that point, the motor gave up and let gravity take over. The top collapsed and flopped onto the windshield frame like a withered, white rose.

"Click the clasp like this," I instructed Laverne.

I lined up the canvas top's clip to the frame's fastener and snapped it into place. Laverne tried to do the same on her side, but ended up breaking another nail.

"Dang it! I wonder if the price of beauty is worth it, Val. Another blasted trip to Beauty Nail. I'd probably own a ski resort in Vail if I wasn't addicted to gel nails."

I climbed out of the old Ford and studied the red polished claws I'd gotten to impress a man I'd probably never see again.

"How do I get rid of these things, Laverne?"

She swung her long, skinny legs out of the car and hoisted herself to her feet.

"You've got another two weeks on those, sugar. Don't waste it. I'll glue this one back on until Winky can get my car fixed."

"Oh crap! I forgot! I'll call Winnie again. Maybe she can drop Winky by when she gets off today at three."

"That'd be swell."

Laverne looked at her watch.

"You know, that's just an hour from now. How about I come inside and make us a pot of coffee? You still look a bit shaken up. Maybe you ought not be alone."

"Uh...sure."

I let Laverne in and pointed to the coffee pot. I sat on a stool at the bar and dialed Winnie while the nosy lady from Vegas rifled through my kitchen cabinets.

"Winnie? Hey. Can you talk?"

"Latrina?"

"No. It's *me. Val!*"

"Sorry! It's just...well, Latrina left in a huff right after you did. I thought maybe it was her calling."

"It's okay. Winnie, do you know what Latrina does on that computer? I mean, what are all those charts and tables I saw her working on?"

"Oh. That's dog track stuff. She and Loo are down at Derby Lane betting every day that place is open. She's gone off there now to catch the afternoon matinee."

"Okay. That makes sense, thanks. Can I talk to Winky now?"

"He's in the john."

"Oh. Uh...just curious. Do Latrina and Loo know a guy named Mickie?"

"I don't know. What's he look like?"

"Hard to miss. He's got an eye patch and a gold front tooth."

"Hmm. We got a couple of regulars match that description."

What? "Okay. He's missing a finger?"

"Got a few of those, too."

"Really?"

"Yeah."

"He plays a guitar?"

"Not sure. How would I know?"

Good point. "Winnie, do you think Loo might be capable of chopping off a guy's finger?"

"Oh. Hmmm. Well, you know he's always throwing knives at the rats in the kitchen. His aim's pretty good, too. It's gross, but he likes to cut the rats' heads off after he stabs 'em. Loo told me one time that was his way of 'getting even with the rats.' I saw him one time—"

"So I guess that's a 'yes.'"

"For sure. I could definitely see Loo cutting off somebody's finger. Especially if there's money in it for him."

"Really?"

"Val, I heard them talking. Loo and Latrina are just about flat broke. I'm not supposed to tell anybody, but lately they've been making me 'recycle' the coffee *and* the creamers. They say reheating takes out the germs, but I don't know if I believe all that."

I fought back a gag. "Thanks, Winnie."

"Sure. Anytime. But what good is a finger, Val? Can you sell them on the black market or something?"

WTF. "I don't think so. But this one had a gold ring on it. That might go a ways toward paying off gambling debts."

"Oh. I get it."

"Winnie, why don't you just bring Winky by when you get off work?"

"Okay. Will do."

I clicked off the phone. Laverne set a cup of coffee on the counter in front of me. I watched the cream swirl around in the mug and fought back a retch.

"What's the matter, sugar?" Laverne asked. "I thought you liked it with cream."

Chapter Twenty-Seven

Couches Today was still holding my new sofa for ransom, so Laverne and I sat on stools at the kitchen breakfast bar. While we waited for Winnie to come by with Winky, Laverne drank coffee. I sipped on iced tea.

"I still can't for the life of me figure out how that finger ended up in *my* couch, Laverne. Life can really suck sometimes."

Laverne reached a long, thin arm over and patted my back.

"Sorry, sugar. Hey, do you have a picture of it?"

"The couch?"

"No. The finger."

"Really? You want to see it?"

"Hey, indulge an old lady. Cheap thrills are the only ones I can afford anymore."

"Okay, but it's gross."

I searched my cell phone for the picture. I handed it to Laverne. She eyed it and grimaced.

"Eeew. You're right. Mighty gruesome."

"Told you."

Suddenly her horsey face brightened. "But that's a nice manicure!"

A horn sounded in the driveway. I climbed off my stool and shuffled to the front door. Winnie drove up in a bluish-gray Dodge Caravan at least a decade older than she was. She hit the brakes. A second later, the side door opened and all three stooges tumbled out like a low-bud-get clown-car act. Winky ran toward my front door like he needed to use the crapper, but he stopped a foot in front of me, his eyes as big as saucers.

"Val, you won't believe what I just did!"

I wasn't at all sure I wanted to know. I turned my face sideways and braced for the words that would surely come, whether I wanted them to or not.

"What?" I said out of the side of my mouth.

"I found an insurance policy. For a million bucks!"

My head snapped back to face him.

"What? What are you talking about, Winky?"

Winnie sidled up to Winky and punched him on the arm.

"Val, he told me he was going to the toilet, but he didn't. He snuck into the kitchen and went through Loo's papers. He's gonna get me fired!"

"Now I didn't do nothin' of the sort," Winky said. "That there policy was sittin' right on top of his desk. And I won't say a word about it if you don't want me to, darlin'."

"But you just did!" Winnie punched Winky on the arm again.

"Oh. Yeah. Sorry 'bout that."

"Why would he have his insurance papers out?" I asked. "Is he planning on making a claim?"

"Maybe," Winnie said. "I've noticed a few things missing lately."

"Like what?"

"Well, like the dishwasher...and the steam cleaner."

"It wasn't like they were using them anyway," I said sourly.

"They're really hurting for cash," Winnie said. "I heard them talking about not being able to make their mortgage payments."

"That sounds like motivation enough to cut off a finger to get the gold ring," Laverne said.

"Bingo," I said.

"Or maybe Bingo Bob," Laverne said.

I looked over at the idiot-savant. Her donkey eyes were staring up at a point to her right. Whether she was contemplating the man's motive or merely lost in space was anyone's guess.

MY LIFE WAS HANGING on by a thread attached to five needles—none of which was sharp enough to puncture wet tissue paper. Winnie, Winky, Jorge, Goober and Laverne were sitting in a circle on my living room floor, trying to devise a plan to find out what Loo and Latrina were up to. I stood in the kitchen watching them, my hand on the freezer handle, contemplating whether or not it was TNT time. I was pretty sure it was.

"I've seen Loo and Bingo Bob hanging out at Cigar Daddy's," Goober said.

"I could go over there," Winnie offered.

"No. Not plausible. A woman would never hang out there," Goober countered. "Besides, they know you. It would have to be someone they didn't know—or couldn't recognize. If I had a disguise, I could try to eavesdrop on their conversation."

"How about that Über-dog scam you got goin'," Winky suggested.

Goober smoothed his moustache with his thumb and index finger as he considered the idea. The other four stared at him like lost groupies, waiting patiently for their fearless leader to announce the way to salvation.

"It would seem more authentic if I actually had a customer of the canine persuasion," Goober said finally.

"If you mean you need a dog, I think I can help with that," Laverne chimed in.

"Yes, that's precisely what I mean. What do you have in mind, Laverne?"

"Well, my next-door neighbor has a bulldog named Buster."

"I was hoping for something a little less aggressive. A more passive pooch, if you will."

Laverne nodded agreeably. "Oh, he's a real pussycat when you know how to handle him. I got him to stop barking all day with one little trick."

Goober's left eyebrow raised an inch. "Really? What was that?"

"I found out he likes beer."

"That could work," Jorge said.

"Shore could," Winky agreed. "What's the worst that could happen?"

Everyone turned to face me. I shrugged and nodded. With no other options, the worst that could happen didn't seem all that bad.

AFTER EVERYONE LEFT, I checked my phone. There was a text from Tom. It read, "I'm worried about you. Stay out of trouble, please. Call me."

A shiver ran up my spine. *What does he know?* It was almost as if Tom was spying on me through my window. How could he know what I was up to? I tapped a finger on my chin until an idea shook loose. *Oh yeah. Tom's little pal Jorge.* The thought of him invading my privacy made me madder than a bucktoothed Billy goat. I punched speed dial.

"Val! Finally!"

"Finally what, Tom? I don't appreciate you having your little minion Jorge spying on me."

"What are you talking about?"

I frowned. "Don't give me that crap or I'm hanging up."

"Okay, okay. How did you know?"

"I'm a freaking *detective*, remember? You called me one yourself. What do you want, Tom?"

"I want to make sure you don't do anything stupid."

"*Me* do something stupid? You're one to talk."

"I know. Look, just give me a chance to explain. About the baby. It's complicated."

"Well, make it uncomplicated."

"Okay," Tom said. "It wasn't my baby."

I blanched. "Then why is Lieutenant Jergen so sure it is?"

"Because I let him believe it."

"Why would you do that?"

"Please, don't make me do this over the phone."

"Do what? Break up with me? Tell me about your affair?"

"What?" Tom yelled. "No! I meant don't make me—"

A will inside me stronger than I knew took possession of my thumb and made it push the little red circle on my phone.

The line went dead.

I'd heard so many excuses in my life, I didn't have time for one more.

Chapter Twenty-Eight

I was holed up inside Chocolateers with my eyes on the door and my mouth full of chocolate. If Goober didn't show up soon, I was going to have to go buy bigger pants. Two peanut clusters and an almond bark later, I watched him shuffle by the glass storefront. Buster the bulldog was passed out inside the patched-up, moon-lander stroller. His tongue hung out of his drooling chops like a huge, pink slug and dangled halfway down to the sidewalk.

Goober touched his thumb to his middle finger as he passed. Everything was A-Okay. Go time. My phone rang.

"Goober One to Goober Two. Approaching target. Out."

"Roger that. Good luck," I whispered and clicked off the phone.

"What was that?" Jack asked.

"Looked like a guy and his dog," I said casually.

"Was the dog dead?"

"I hope not."

Jack came and stood beside me at the front of the store. Through the shop window, between a huge, maniacal-looking stuffed bunny and big baskets of chocolate Easter goodies, we watched Goober carry out the plan. He strolled over nonchalantly and took a seat at a table adjacent to Loo and Bingo Bob. They'd arrived at Cigar Daddy's five minutes and four chocolate-mint patties ago. I'd texted Goober the moment they'd shown up.

Yesterday, I'd begged Goober not to wear the Burger King crown to the stakeout. He'd complied with my request, but had gone rogue and upped the ante with a hideous, dime-store false nose and eyeglasses combo. At least he'd removed the moustache. *That* he hadn't needed to fake. Combined with his improvised derby hat, Goober looked like Mr. Peanut's psychotic cousin, Looney Legume.

"Now I've seen everything," Jack said.

How had my life led up to this moment? I thought about my college degree. My time in Europe. My professional writing career. Like Jack, I'd seen everything, too. And like the rest of it, this moment would end up one day as mere dust in the gutter. I hoped it would be soon. I closed my eyes, took a deep breath and buoyed myself with false hope.

"Don't you know, Jack? Dog-sitting is a growing cottage industry. Rich people getting flunkies to push their pampered pooches around in strollers seems like the next logical step."

"I guess anything's possible."

Jack went back to work behind the counter. I put my nose to the glass and cringed as Goober leaned over the stroller and his fake nose and glasses fell to the sidewalk. He yanked them off the ground, slapped them on his face and glanced around. He looked my way and nodded. Not knowing what else to do, I nodded back. He pulled a newspaper out of the stroller, sat back down and pretended to read it, even though it was upside down. I glanced over at Loo and Bingo Bob. So far, they hadn't noticed. They were busy yacking it up between puffs of thick, yellow smoke. I could almost smell the disgusting blend of cherry and tobacco farts through the glass.

Goober laid the newspaper down on the table. I held my breath. He whipped out a bright-yellow funnel from his stroller and put it to his ear. I shook my head in disbelief.

"Why didn't you just ask them to talk into a microphone?" I muttered.

"What did you say?" Jack asked from across the shop.

I turned to face him. "Nothing. Just talking to myself."

Jack raised his eyebrows at me. I turned back to the window just in time to see all hell break loose. *Crap!*

Loo was on his feet, yelling at Goober. I grabbed the display Easter bunny by the neck and watched in horror as Loo reared back and punched Goober in the plastic nose. Goober's head shot sideways. The fake eyeglasses and proboscis went flying in the air. By some idiotic stroke of fate, the plastic funnel landed right on Buster's head like a dunce cap. The bulldog woke from his beer-induced coma, lunged out of the stroller and latched his jaws squarely on Loo's right calf. Loo kicked like a mule. Buster hung on like a bad debt.

While Loo did the mamba with Buster, Bingo Bob scrambled to the top of the metal table. He bent over, picked up a black plastic ashtray and threw it at Buster. It hit the bulldog on his right rear flank. Buster let go of Loo and made a lunge at Bingo Bob. The jerk's smug Elvis sneer disappeared, replaced by wild panic. He took a step backward, lost his balance, flailed his arms wildly and fell off the table. Bingo Bob landed hard on his butt on the sidewalk. His hands flew up to his throat. I couldn't tell if he was protecting himself from Buster or he'd swallowed his stogie. The table rolled in front of him, blocking my view.

I looked around. Goober and the stroller were gone. Someone yelled something I couldn't make out. All at once, Laverne, Winky and Jorge came out from behind cars and corners and scattered like cockroaches. A flash of movement caught my eye. I looked down. Buster trotted by the store window dragging half a pants leg in his mouth. I gasped and took a step back.

"You okay, Val?" Jack asked.

I suddenly remembered where I was.

"Oh. Sure, Jack."

I let loose of my stranglehold on the psychotic-faced Easter rabbit. His twisted head flopped to one side. Jack frowned at me.

"Sorry about the rabbit."

I peeked out the window again. Loo and Bingo Bob had gotten to their feet. They dusted themselves off and disappeared inside Cigar Daddy's.

"What are you looking at?" Jack asked.

"Nothing. Gotta go. See you next time."

I snuck out of Chocolateers and ran like a chocolate-fueled fool the block and a half to Maggie. I'd parked her in the alley behind The Deet, in back of Winnie's Dodge. Winnie had stayed in the van to make sure our cars didn't get towed. Now she was going to get a lesson in driving a getaway vehicle. I turned the corner to the alley and saw Jorge's tattle-tail butt disappear inside the van's side door. He'd already ratted out our plan to Tom, so I figured there was no harm in letting him tag along. I hadn't planned on this turning into a flipping fiasco. I should have known better.

I stopped running and huffed and puffed up to the van.

"Everybody in?" I asked.

"No sign of Goober," Winnie reported.

I looked behind the van. Laverne was in Maggie's passenger seat, holding Buster in her lap.

"We can't wait for him, Winnie. I don't want to be spotted with the attack dog."

"Okay," Winnie said. "Lead the way."

I pulled out and drove down to Beach Drive. Winnie, Winky and Jorge followed behind us in the van. I took a left and cruised by the park to the Vinoy Hotel. I hooked a left on Fifth Avenue North and headed west toward the beach. The whole while, Laverne and I sat in silence, listening to Buster hassle and whine as I headed toward home. We were halfway to the beach when the phone rang. I put it on speaker.

"Goober One to Goober Two."

"Woo hoo!"

Laverne and I both hooted for joy, then broke out in nervous laughter.

"What the hell's so funny?" Goober asked. "My butt was on the line."

"Sorry, Goober. We're just relieved you survived. Are you okay?"

"Affirmative. With intelligence gathered."

"What?"

"Mission accomplished. I got what we came for."

"What did you find out?"

"They're planning on burning Water Loo's to the ground."

Chapter Twenty-Nine

Insurance fraud? *Geez!* I was back to those two bad choices; call the cops or call an attorney. I was about to stick a blind finger in the yellow pages when I heard a sharp rapping at my door. I looked out the peephole and saw a frizzy-haired man at the door and a bright-yellow Hummer in the driveway. I set my jaw to scowl and opened the door.

"Mr. Finkerman, what are you doing here?"

"Slow day. I came by to personally serve you with Mr. Michaels' lawsuit myself. I thought I'd give you one last chance to pony up some cash before this crap hits the fan."

"Your client went to the police. The crap's already hit the fan."

"What? That little son of a—"

"How did you find my home?"

Finkerman laughed.

"You're kidding, right? This is the internet age, grandma. Give anyone half a name or most of a phone number, and you can find where they're hiding, even if it's on Mars."

"Oh."

"Are you going to let me in? We can either discuss terms now, or at the courthouse."

I opened the door wide enough to let him pass.

"You know I didn't do it."

"Yeah, well. Boo hoo. Somebody's got to pay my rent."

"What if I could get you a bigger fish to fry?"

Finkerman looked around my place. I watched his high hopes fade to middle class.

"What kind of fish?"

"A million-dollar fish."

Finkerman's lips curled upward.

"I'm listening."

"I know who cut off Mickie's finger. It was Loo...of Water Loo's Restaurant."

"All right. So, this Loo. Has he got more money than you?"

"Don't you want to hear the story of why I think he did it?"

"Irrelevant. Unless he's got more money than you. I don't ask my questions willy-nilly, Ms. Fremden. Priority one is to crack the biggest nest egg."

"Wow. At least you're honest about it."

"No point beating around a bush if it's full of deadbeat birds. So, is this Water Loo's place worth a million? Fine dining, perhaps?"

"Not exactly."

"So where's the million dollars? Land? Building value?"

"No. It's more like...a million dollars in insurance coverage."

"Worth nothing unless the place is destroyed."

"But that's just it. The restaurant is a month away from foreclosure. A friend of mine heard Loo talking about torching the place for the payoff."

Finkerman scowled, then smiled wryly.

"Ah. Good old insurance fraud. The last bastion of a broke scoundrel. There's good money in it, if you can pull it off."

"So you'll consider dropping me for Loo?"

"Where's your proof. Do you have his computer with the plan outlined on it?"

"No."

"Notes in his handwriting?"

"No."

"Video?"

"No."

Finkerman shook his head.

"A tape recording, then?"

"No. Just the word of my friend."

Finkerman blew out a disappointed breath.

"Is this person of upstanding character? Would a jury believe him or her?"

I pictured Goober with his Burger King crown. Crap! "Not exactly. What other kind of evidence would work?"

Finkerman scowled again.

"You've got nothing then, I take it."

"Not at the moment. But with your help, maybe we could get it on tape. I know a waitress at the restaurant. She could help."

Finkerman looked around my place again.

"Can't you even afford a couch?"

"No," I lied.

"Okay. I'll give you a bug and two days."

"A bug?"

"A micro-sized recorder, Ms. Fremden. Smaller than a pack of gum. Here, look."

Finkerman reached in his pocket and pulled out a device that looked like a computer thumb drive.

"This little baby is the spy's dream come true. Looks like a thumb drive, but it's eight gigabytes of video *and* audio surveillance. Motion activated, too. Brilliant."

"What should I do with it?"

"Plant it where you can catch them talking. Where do they congregate? Conduct business? Chew the fat?"

"Uh...at the restaurant. They sit in a corner booth, mostly."

"Perfect. Just put it on the table. Inside a salt shaker is best. Doesn't mess up the lens, usually. It'll come on automatically when it detects motion or sound. Record something incriminating and bring it back to me."

Finkerman handed me the device. It really did look just like a thumb drive.

"That's amazing."

"I've always got one running. In my line of work, I never know when some juicy bit of news will spill. You really do need to get into the twenty-first century, Ms. Fremden."

AFTER FINKERMAN LEFT, I went out in the backyard and stared out at the water. Even if I was lucky enough to get Loo on tape plotting arson to commit insurance fraud, given Finkerman's integrity, it might end up doing zilch to get me off the hook about the finger. It was a long-shot that Loo would mention it anyway. Why would he bother talking about cutting off a finger when he had a new, million-dollar scheme to plot out?

Crap! How did that finger get from Mickie, to Loo, then to my couch? What if it wasn't Mickie's finger at all? What if the DNA came back positive on the dumpster guy? I didn't know squat about him. Maybe I should find out what I can....

I took a long shot and called a guy I knew at the county morgue. He'd helped me claim Glad's body last year. I was hoping that maybe he would do me another favor. It was worth a try.

"Hello, could I speak with Mr. Darren Dudley?"

"Who's calling, please."

"Um...Val Fremden?"

"Valiant Stranger! Is that you?"

"Yes. You remember me?"

"How could I forget? The one that got away."

"Not easy in your line of work."

"Ha ha! Stop with that awesome sense of humor of yours. Don't make me miss you more."

"You *miss* me?"

"You were the best date I've had in years."

"Out of how many?"

"Do relatives count?"

"They do where I come from."

"Stop it! You're too much!"

"I can't believe you remember me, Darren. I'm sorry to call asking for another favor, but I could really use your help."

"Uh oh. Here it comes. What's up?"

"It's just that...well...I'm in a bit of a pickle. Did you happen to see a guy come in that was missing a couple of fingers?"

"You talking about the dumpster guy?"

"Yes. It's a long story, but I found a finger with a ring on it. The initials were either HM or WH. I heard the guy's name was Warren Harris. Can you confirm that?"

"Yeah. I'm pretty positive that's the guy."

"How come?"

"His name was tattooed across his back."

"Oh."

"Was he missing an index finger?"

"He was missing every finger except his thumbs."

"Oh my gawd! How did *that* happen?"

"My theory? He was dumpster diving. He rigged the lid open, but when he went to haul himself out, he knocked the lid closed. It landed on his hands and cut his fingers to the bone."

"Did that kill him?"

"Probably got knocked out when the lid hit. Concussion, loss of blood most likely."

"Did they find his other fingers?"

"Nope. Inside the bellies of a few stray dogs and cats, most likely."

"Yuck. The finger I found was wrapped in a cloth. Probably not his, then."

"Where'd you find it?"

"In an alley. I mean, in a couch that was in an alley."

"I won't ask what you were doing on a couch in an alley."

"Thanks."

"Hmmm. Wrapped in a cloth, huh? It still could be this guy's finger. You know, people like macabre souvenirs. Maybe someone picked it up, held onto it until it started to stink, then ditched it in the couch. Where was the couch?"

"In the alley between Sixth and Seventh avenues."

"Hmm. Let me look. Yeah. His toe tag says "found in dumpster off of Ninth Avenue and Second Street. That's pretty close by, isn't it?"

"Yes. But Darren, are you...I mean...you're looking at his body right now?"

"Yeah. Just wanted to be sure about the tattoo. Wanna go out again? Give it another try?"

"Thanks, but...."

"You still seeing that cop?"

"I was until recently."

"Then let's go out. Take it slow. If it's just friendship, so be it."

"Why would you want to go out with me again?"

"Because you, Valiant Stranger, are the most interesting woman I've ever met."

"It's easy to compete with cadavers."

"Ha ha! Come on, what do you say?"

"I'm kind of in a jam right now. I'll call you when I'm up for it."

"Fair enough. Good luck. Call me anytime, okay?"

"Okay. Thanks, Darren."

I clicked off the phone and washed my hands. I grabbed my purse and headed for the door. I was going to need some more figurines.

Chapter Thirty

"Did you bring the salt shaker?"

"Oh crap. I'm sorry, Val. I knew I was forgetting something."

Winnie's features scrunched together and her head drooped. We were inside her van, parked in my driveway. It was 6:30 a.m. We were going over our scheme to catch Loo's arson plan, on tape this time. As I held the recording device in my hand and explained it to Winnie, I felt a little like *James Bond*—if he had boobs, trepidation, PMS and a conscience, that is.

"It's all set to automatically record. You don't have to do a thing. Just get it in the salt shaker. Do you think it will fit?"

I handed Winnie the micro recorder. She laid it along the length of her index finger and nodded confidently.

"It should work. It's shorter than my finger. The salt shakers are exactly as long as my finger."

"How do you know that?"

"Oh. Well...there's lots of down time between customers."

Okay. "So, you think it'll be safe inside the salt shaker? I mean, if someone uses it?"

"Yeah. I think we're cool. Loo sold the stove yesterday. I saw some guys hauling it out last night. Unless somebody likes salt in their coffee, we should be good."

"And you think you can get the recorder into the shaker and set it on the table in the corner booth without Loo or Latrina noticing?"

Winnie looked up at me.

"I'm not a child, Val."

"I know. I'm sorry. It's just...this could turn dangerous. I don't want you to get caught."

"Trust me, Val. It should be no problem. We're supposed to open at 7:30, but if I didn't go in early and get the place going, I don't think we'd open before ten. They're always running late."

"Okay. Good. But promise me, if you hit a snag you'll text me. I'm only a few minutes away."

"Right. I promise."

I hugged Winnie, climbed out of the van and shut the door. Winnie sat frozen in the driver's seat like a worried, plus-sized mannequin. I tapped on the window.

"Hey. Are you okay?"

Winnie rolled the window down a crack.

"Yeah. Just nervous. I've never done anything like this before."

"Me either. You know, you don't have to do—"

"No. I want to. You've been good to me and Winky. Not many people treat us with respect. I want to return the favor."

Hot tears filled my eyes.

"Thank you, Winnie. You could be saving me from jail time. I'm not keeping score, but if this goes off as planned, I'll be the one owing *you*. Big time."

Winnie grinned. "Yeah. Okay."

I smiled and gave her a thumb's up.

"Good luck, Winnie. And remember, I'm right here if you need me."

Winnie nodded, looked straight ahead and put the van in drive.

"I've got this," she said to herself.

I watched the van's taillights disappear down the street. The sky was just starting to pink up from the coming sunrise. A lump formed in my throat as I thought about Winnie and her day ahead. Like Goober had yesterday, she was putting her butt on the line for me. It was both scary and wonderful to know there were people on the planet who thought I was worth the risk.

I went inside and fixed a cappuccino. Winnie texted me ten minutes later. It read: "Shaker in place." I sent back an emoji "thumbs up" symbol.

The trap was set. Now all we needed were the rats.

AT NOON, I GOT A CALL from Winnie.

"Val, there's a problem."

The hair on my neck prickled.

"Are you okay?"

"Yeah. But I'm not at work."

"What happened?"

"I set the salt shaker up with no problem. But when they came in this morning, Loo and Latrina were at each other's throats again. They kept arguing and acting real paranoid, you know? Bingo Bob came in, and then they all three kept looking at me funny. I don't know what I was doing wrong. Maybe I looked at them too much. Anyway, they told me to make a pot of coffee and go home. I made the coffee and carried it over to the booth. I poured them each a cup and tried to take the salt shaker, but they had papers piled on top of it. I'm sorry, Val."

"Don't worry. We'll just pick it up in the morning. It might actually be good. We can record them all evening this way."

"Oh. Okay. Thanks for understanding, Val."

"Thank you for helping, Winnie. Call me in the morning and I'll go with you to pick it up."

"Thanks. That place is kinda creepy in the dark."

"It's kinda creepy in the daytime, too."

I MADE MYSELF A GLASS of iced tea and went out in the backyard. I unfolded a lawn chair next to the old RV and pretended I was camping out with Glad. I spent the evening in silence, watching the pelicans and ibis fly to their roosts as the stars blinked on one-by-one like night-lights illuminating their way home. Right before dusk a dragonfly landed on my hand. I reached up to touch my mom's pendant on a chain around my neck and the dragonfly flew away. I took it as a good sign.

AT THE CRACK OF DAWN, I got up and pulled on my stealth spy outfit—black sweatpants and a dark-gray t-shirt. I perked a cappuccino and googled the news. The headline read: "Major Fire on Gulf Boulevard." My gut fell a foot closer to the floor. I scanned the article. No address was mentioned, but there's no denying it. The gut knows what the gut knows.

Winnie's headlights flashed in my front window. I inched into my sneakers, sprinted outside and jumped in the van.

"Morning, Winnie. Let's get going. I think we should hurry."

"Why?"

There was no point getting Winnie upset over nothing. I made up an excuse.

"I ate some bad seafood last night and I'm not feeling so great."

"Oh. Okay. I'll step on it."

Winnie hit the gas. The g-force sent me tumbling backwards.

"Oh no! I'm sorry!"

"Don't be. Put the pedal to the metal."

"What?"

"Mash the gas pedal to the floorboard."

"Oh. Got it!"

The van turned right onto Gulf Boulevard on two wheels. After a couple of blocks, I could already see the glow of the fire in the purple morning twilight. It formed an eerily beautiful, light-orange backdrop for the flashing red-and-blue lights of every cop car and firetruck in Pinellas County.

"Wow! What's going on, Val?"

"I'm not sure. Tell you what. Turn right here. Let's take the back way on Boca Ciega and avoid this mess."

I pointed the way and we skirted the main arteries already clogging with gawkers and early-morning commuters. We parked in front of a house a block behind Water Loo's and stared through the windshield as a firetruck shot a plume of water at the smoking hull that was once the most disgusting coffee house in the world. Water Loo's had gone down in flames.

"Oh no! Your salt shaker!" Winnie cried.

"Yeah. Crap. But there goes your job, too. I'm sorry."

"It wasn't your fault."

"Yours either."

I blew out a big breath.

"Hey. Since we've both got nothing better to do now, let's go get a closer look."

The Dodge's worn-out struts squeaked in protest as we climbed out. We walked toward the blaze until we reached a yellow tape stretched around the scene. It fluttered in the pre-dawn breeze, daring us not to cross it. Winnie and I joined the crowd of dozens of pyromaniacal onlookers mesmerized by the smoldering heap. Paramedics arrived a few minutes later. Right behind the ambulance I spotted a lemon-yellow hummer. A few seconds later, I saw Finkerman's frizzy brown hair bobbing in the crowd. He walked up to me and handed me a card, his eyes already on the lookout for the next empty palm.

"Lady, if you feel injured or traumatized by this in any way, give me a call. There's cash in catastrophe."

Finkerman shot me a smarmy smile. It disappeared the instant he recognized me.

"What are *you* doing here?"

"I could ask you the same thing, but I already know the answer."

Finkerman looked over at the blaze, then back to me.

"Don't tell me. Is *this* the place?"

"Yep."

"The *million-dollar policy* place?"

"Yep."

Finkerman scanned the charred remains and grinned with the right side of his mouth.

"Okay, Ms. Fremden. You've got my attention. Tell me what I need to know right now and we might be able to scratch your name off the Michaels' lawsuit and write in a new one."

"What do you need to know?"

"How much are you worth?"

"Geez, you get to the point, don't you. I don't know for sure."

"Guestimate it. As a percentage of a million."

"Not even twenty-five percent."

"Okay. So we've established Loo's the bigger cash prize. But still, you had possession of the finger. That's troubling. A guy like me could plow that fact into the ground until a nice nuisance settlement sprouted up."

"Yeah, I know."

"Oh. Yeah, I guess you do. Possession of said missing body part is usually good for at least ten grand, Ms. Fremden. But I'm willing to consider dropping it for this 'bigger fish,' as you say. Just hand over the recording."

"Yes. That sounds good. There's only one problem."

"What's that?"

"The recorder was in there."

I nodded toward the burnt-out husk of the building. Finkerman stomped his foot, then regained his composure. His eyes looked up and to the left as his brain concocted another scheme.

"So, you've got no evidence. How inconvenient for you *and* me. But I might still be able to make this work. You're worth a quarter mil. How do I know you didn't set that fire yourself, you little arsonist, you?"

"What are you talking about?"

"Let's see. You knew about the insurance money and the arson plan. You approached me, leveraging it to get you off the hook with the finger dealio. And gee, I just happened to run into you in the parking lot while the place was going up in flames. Arsonists do love to admire their own handiwork."

"That's...that's despicable!"

"I know. And I've got it all on tape." Finkerman patted his pocket. "Looks like you might be in even hotter water now, Ms. Fremden. I'll be in touch. And by the way, you owe me for the recording device. I'll send you a bill."

"You're ridiculous! Isn't talking to me about all that stuff some kind of conflict of interest?"

"Lady, if there's money in it, I got no conflict. And you? Unlike me, you've got no proof."

I grabbed for Finkerman's shirt pocket, but he covered it with his hand. He smiled like Snidely Whiplash and disappeared into the crowd. A second later, Winky emerged from the same throng of people gawking at the catastrophe. He sidled up next to me and bit into a boiled egg, as if he was enjoying popcorn and a show.

"Hey, Val pal! Can you believe that? Some people's got some rotten luck, you know?"

"Yeah. I know."

He took another bite of egg. His nonchalance aggravated me.

"What are you doing here, Winky?"

"Came to see Winnie. She was antsy about something all day yesterday."

"Yeah? What?"

"She didn't say. But I could tell somethin' was getting her all riled up. Left without sayin' a word this morning. I hitched a ride over to make sure she was okay."

His surprising compassion softened my attitude.

"You really like her, don't you."

"Yep. She's a good egg."

Winky caught himself off guard with his own joke and laughed.

"Good egg. Now that there's funny."

"Yeah."

Winky raised the last bite of boiled egg up like a toast to the blackened building.

"To Water Loo's. I'll miss your booze. But Loo and Latrina? Not you twos."

"You're the quintessential country poet, Winky. I bet Glad loved the poem you recited at her memorial service. I never thanked you for that."

"It's never too late to say thanks, Val."

"Okay. Thanks."

Winky put his arm around me. We watched the firetruck put out the last flame. Suddenly Winky's arm flew off my shoulder. He jerked back, raised both fists in air and beat them down on an imaginary table.

"Gaul dang it!"

"What's wrong?"

"There goes my free clothes box!"

Yep. And my *get-out-of-jail-free card.*

Chapter Thirty-One

"Have you seen Winnie?" Winky hollered.

The crowd at Water Loo's last-ever barbecue had doubled. It was getting hard to hear above the din. I cupped my hand to Winky's ear and yelled.

"She was right beside me. I talked to this guy Finkerman, and she disappeared. But she's got to be in the crowd somewhere. Or back at the Dodge. Want me to show you where we parked?"

"Sure. I could use a nap."

I took a step in the direction of the van and found myself staring at a chest-full of blue. The face attached to the chest was handsome, with sandy blond hair and sea-green eyes.

"Hiya, Tom-Tom," Winky said.

Tom nodded at Winky, then locked eyes with me. I looked away and watched Winky pull a pink boiled egg out of a pocket in his cargo shorts. He tapped the egg on his forehead with enough force to crack the shell. I felt Tom's hands softly grip my upper arms.

"Val, what are you doing here?"

I shot him a hard look and pulled away.

"Trying to save my own hide. With no help from *you*, thanks very much."

"Look, Val. I told you it would be worse if I got involved. Why won't you believe me?"

"Because I just *don't*. You're selfish, Tom. You put your own needs above mine. I'm in big trouble. I need help. Where are you? Off with someone else!"

"Val, I—"

"I thought I had a plan. But it just went up in flames. And you won't...you're not...."

I burst into tears. *Darn it!* I didn't want Tom to see me cry. I looked over at Winky. He'd finished shelling the egg. Flakes of pink shell littered the asphalt like hobo snow. He reached into his shorts pocket. I gasped.

"Where did you get that?" I yelled.

Winky looked at me like a deer in the headlights. "Huh?"

I ran over and snatched the salt shaker from Winky's hand. Inside was a little contraption that looked like a computer thumb drive.

"Yes!!!" I screamed.

I grabbed Winky and kissed him on the lips. He nearly fell backwards.

"Where did you find this?"

"Well, I kinda lifted it from Loo's last night. If I'd a knowed you loved salt shakers so much, Val, I'd a snatched you one, too."

"Why did you take it?"

"I ain't no thief, if that's what you mean. I just love me some Easter eggs. Every year, Winn Dixie down the road has 'em cheap as dirt. I bought me a dozen yesterday on my way to see Winnie at work. She weren't there. So, I sat myself down at the booth, like always. Somebody'd left a pile a papers all over it. I shoved 'em to the side and started eatin' my eggs. All of a sudden, old Loo hisself come over and tole me to get lost. Said Winnie wasn't coming back 'til tomorrow. Val, I needed the salt to eat my eggs. What's a feller to do? I stuck the shaker in my shorts pocket. I was gonna bring it back. But I guess it don't matter none, no more anyhoo."

"Oh, it matters. It matters plenty! Thank you, Winky!"

I grabbed Winky's hand and jumped up and down.

"Val, what's going on?" Tom asked.

My mood shifted faster than a rabbit's romance. I whipped around to face him.

"You tell me, Tom, and I'll tell you."

Tom lowered his head and bit his lower lip. He turned and took a step to leave, then turned back.

"I'll call you. No. I'll come over tonight after work and explain it all."

Before I could answer, Tom disappeared into the crowd. Winnie walked up. She looked distraught.

"Val, it's hopeless and it's all my fault!"

I held up the recorder. "Winnie, we've got it!"

"What? How?"

"Your boyfriend saved the day."

I waved a hand at Winky. He grinned like a bashful gnome.

"Shucks. Wat'n nothin'."

"I'll explain on the way, Winnie. Let's get the hell out of here."

WINNIE DROPPED ME AT my house. Halleluiah, I had the tape! With any luck, it contained the evidence I needed to get Finkerman off my butt! I had my fingers on my phone to call him when I remembered something; the sleazebag's loyalty blew with the wind. I needed someone looking out for *me* and *me alone*. I paced around my kitchen. Something on a shelf caught my eye. It was that old phone book I'd found when I'd cleaned out my parents' thirty years' worth of hoarder debris.

I flipped through the yellow pages. There were over a hundred pages of attorneys! *Crap!* I closed my eyes, touched my dragonfly pendant for luck, fanned the pages, and stuck my finger on a name.

"Bernard Charles, you'd better be good," I said to myself as I dialed.

A woman answered.

"Bernard Charles, civil defense attorney. May I help you?"

"I'd like to make an appointment?"

"Certainly. What's your availability?"

"Um...now? Anytime?"

"You're in luck. Mr. Charles has an opening at 3:30 today. Initial consultation, correct?"

"Yes."

"That will be two hundred for the hour. We accept credit cards and Paypal only. No checks. Do you understand the terms?"

"Yes."

"And you still want to come?"

"Uh...yes."

"Very good. Who shall I say is coming?

"Val Fremden."

"That name sounds familiar. Did you say Val Shremshend?"

My ears grew hot. "No. Val *Fremden*."

"Okay. You're all set. See you this afternoon."

I hung up and immediately felt like I'd made a mistake. How good could this guy be if he could see me on a moment's notice? It was barely after nine o'clock in the morning and I'd already had one hell of a day. I set my phone down and went to the bathroom. It rang as soon as I sat on the toilet. I jumped up and ran for it, yanking my panties up on the way.

"Goober One to Goober Two."

"Goober! Geez!"

"Yeah. Good morning to you, too."

"Sorry. You just...I was just. Never mind. What's up?"

"Val, you're not going to believe this, but I've got Loo in custody."

"What? How? I mean...what? Where are you?"

"Behind The Deet."

"Hold onto him. I'll be right there."

"Don't worry. He's not going anywhere."

I made it downtown in twenty minutes flat. I turned into the alley behind The Deet, but didn't see Goober. I pulled over and climbed out of the car. A peanut-shaped head peeked out from behind a dumpster.

"Over here, Goober Two."

I ran to his side. There, in the grimy corner where the dumpster met the back wall of the liquor store, Loo sat passed out in Goober's industrial-strength stroller. His head lolled to one side. His arms hung limp, knuckles on the pavement. He looked like the biggest, ugliest baby on earth. I turned to Goober.

"Should I even ask?"

"Hey, I didn't kill him, if that's what you mean."

"So he's not dead?"

"Nope. Just passed-out drunk."

I blew out a breath. "Thank goodness. How did this...*happen?*"

Goober scratched his bald head and slapped his baseball cap back over it.

"Well, I ran into Capone this morning. He told me some guy was laying in the alley behind The Deet. Said the guy didn't look like a bum, but he'd been rolled. I thought, hey, I could be a green taxi service. For inebriated clientele, you know? I could push 'em around. Help 'em find their cars and whatnot."

"Okay...I get it. So?"

"So I come down here, and I see this guy laying on his belly. He's got a big bite mark on his calf. I turn him over, it's Loo. I was about to make a run for it when I thought, hey, maybe you and I could take another shot at getting his confession. On tape this time. Besides, it's not like he's going anywhere. He can't even walk."

"Good thinking, Goober. I might have it on tape already. But it wouldn't hurt to get a backup. Besides, what I really need is for him to confess about cutting Mickie's finger off."

"We could work on that. You know, Val, it took me and Capone both to get Loo's fat butt into the stroller. Cost me a dollar and three cigarettes."

I found my wallet and gave Goober three dollars.

"Thanks, Val."

"Sure." I looked back over at Loo. "So why do you think he's *here*. In the alley?"

"He has race tickets in his front pocket. Could a picked a winner yesterday. Down here celebrating, maybe?"

"Celebrating! That's probably it. Did you hear? Water Loo's burned down last night."

"Yeah. Could see the smoke from here."

"Loo would have a million reasons to celebrate that."

Goober eyed the ugly baby and whistled. "Affirmative."

"Do you think we can get him to talk?"

"When me and Capone lifted him, he was lying on an empty bottle of Jack. Go in The Deet and buy a pocket rocket of JD and we might just be able to make this ugly canary to sing."

LOO HELD HIS MOUTH open wide like a baby bird, but it wasn't worms he was after. It was another shot of Jack. We'd convinced the shizzle-faced restaurateur-turned arsonist that we were his new best friends, celebrating his big win at the track. I waved his spent Derby Lane tickets in his face and danced around like there was a party going on.

"Woo hoo! Look at you, it's big-winner Loo!"

Loo grinned and rolled his loopy eyes at me from his seat in the stroller. Goober stood by like a degenerate nanny, an open pint of whiskey in one hand, the cap for it in the other.

"You're a winner, Loo! That dog, *Gold Ring*, just made you a fortune! Have another shot!"

Goober poured a capful of JD and held it over Loo's head. Loo opened wide. Goober poured the booze into his mouth. Loo gulped it down greedily.

"Yes, you're a great big winner, Loo! You bought your tickets with a *gold ring*. How crazy is that?"

"Yeah, preshy craashy," Loo slurred.

"I bet it was hard to get that *gold ring*, huh?"

Loo nodded. "Uh huh."

Goober took a swig out of the JD bottle and poured another capful for Loo.

"What was that, Loo? Come on, tell us how you got the *gold ring* again. That was sooo funny!"

Goober teased Loo with the capful of booze.

"Come on, tell us the story again, Loo! The ring wouldn't come off, remember? You are *sooo* cute and funny!"

"Ah, ya...Loo started. "Couldn't get that...dang thing off. Mickie and his...stupid...big fat finger."

"Fat finger! Sir, pour the man a drink!"

Goober emptied the capful down Loo's gullet. Loo smacked his lips and closed his eyes. *Oh no!* We were almost there. He couldn't pass out now! I kicked the air. Goober caught my drift and kicked the stroller. Loo's bleary eyes opened again. I put on my best party-girl act.

"You're hilarious! Loo! How'd you get that ring off of Mickie's stupid, big fat finger?"

Loo belched loud enough to make a nearby pigeon take wing.

"I cut...I cut that fat jerk's finger off...with my knife."

"Oooh that's so cool, Loo! You're like a strong mountain man. I bet Mickie deserved it, right?"

"Yeah...he did. He owed Bengo Bod money."

"Bengo Bod? Ha ha! That's funny!"

"Bingo Bod."

"So, you gave the finger to Bingo Bob?"

"No. To the little guy...the green dwarf."

What? Oh my gawd! "Oh yeah, sure! The green dwarf. But he told me he couldn't find the finger, Loo. Where'd you put it?"

"In the pocket. Like we said."

"What pocket, Loo?"

"You know. The pocket. But it ain't my fault."

"Oh, nobody's blaming you, Loo. You're the big winner! Buddy, give him another drink."

Goober poured another capful into Loo. His eyes rolled around and his head bobbed.

"Screw the dwarfs," Loo slurred. "Freakin' April fools. You can't trust 'em."

Loo's eyes rolled up in his head. He passed out cold.

"What the hell was all that about?" Goober asked. "Green dwarf?"

I patted my shirt pocket.

"I'm not sure yet, Goober. But I've got it all on tape."

Chapter Thirty-Two

It was fifteen after three when I walked into the law offices of Charles, Charles & Associates. I guess one Charles wasn't enough. The place had a seedy vibe, despite its tasteful, modern furniture and paintings. It felt...*temporary*—as if everything had come as a set out of the back of a truck, and could be packed up and hauled away at a moment's notice. I walked up to a woman behind a thick glass window, like the ones in a doctor's office.

"Miss Fremden?"

"Yes."

"You're early. But Mr. Charles can see you now."

She led me to a door with a plaque that read Bernard Wilton Charles, III, Esq. I didn't want to be impressed, but I was. The receptionist opened the door.

"Ms. Fremden is here to see you."

"Have a seat, Ms. Fremden."

"Thanks for seeing me on short notice."

"You're fortunate. I had a cancellation today. I'd say it was your lucky day, but usually people don't feel that way when they come to see me. I like to think I change people's luck."

"Well, I could certainly use a change of luck."

"Tell me your story and let's see what we can do."

As I laid out my story before this stranger. He studied me and my words with discerning, dark brown eyes the same color as mine. His brown hair showed a touch of grey at the temples. His clean-shaven chin was dimpled in the center, and his lips were full. His thick eyebrows were unruly, but everything else about him was disciplined to the extreme. He wore the well-practiced poker face of every attorney and cop I'd ever seen on TV. He looked tired, yet determined, and his face never betrayed him, even when I said "green dwarf."

"So, let me make sure I've got this straight, Ms. Fremden. First, you found a finger in your abandoned couch, then a dwarf in a Halloween mask broke in and tried to steal the finger. But you'd already given it to the cops. Is that right so far?"

"Yes."

"Okay, then the man who lost the finger...um...."

"Mickie."

"Yes, Mickie with the eye patch and gold tooth. And missing finger, of course. He accused you of putting a bag over his head and chopping his finger off."

"Well...not chopping it off, but telling someone else to."

"Right. Then a woman named Latrina, who sounds like you, said a man named Loo cut the finger off."

"Yes."

"And you and your friend 'Goober' got Loo drunk in a baby stroller and taped his confession with a salt shaker saved from a fire by a man eating Easter eggs."

"Exactly."

"And this Loo character said he gave the finger to a dwarf?"

"A green dwarf. But Loo put it in a pocket and the dwarf didn't find it."

"But you did."

"Yes. In the couch."

"Uh huh. And this green dwarf...is he the same one that broke into your house to steal the finger?"

"I don't know. He was wearing a mask. Alfred E. Neuman?"

Mr. Charles' eyebrows shot up. He reached for the intercom on his desk.

"I see. You're aware, of course, that this sounds a bit...um...*implausible.*"

"Painfully aware."

"Yes. Well, let me just call my secretary."

Oh, crap! "Mr. Charles, I know this sounds crazy...."

"Yes. Hmmm. Well tell me, what exactly did the green dwarf say when he broke in, Ms. Fremden. Did he ask specifically about the finger?"

"Yes. When I told him I didn't have it, he cussed and I kicked him across the room."

"Uh huh."

Aww crap. What did I have to lose now? I closed my eyes and let it rip.

"And then he said, 'Mother of macaroons.'"

I cringed and opened my eyes just in time to see Mr. Charles' eyebrows shoot up again. He punched a button on the intercom on his desk.

"Mr. Charles, I—"

He held a finger up to silence me.

"Miss Chandler...I need you to do something for me. *Immediately...*"

I grabbed my purse and the recording device. I jumped to my feet. *He was calling the nuthouse. I had to make a run for it!* Mr. Charles shook his head and motioned for me to sit.

"...I need you to cancel all of my appointments for this afternoon."

I collapsed back into the chair. Mr. Charles eyed me sternly, then his hard face softened.

"Miss Fremden, you come in here with a story no one on earth would believe. Then you put the cherry on the sundae with a green dwarf who says, 'Mother of macaroons.'"

I cringed. "I know it sounds crazy, but—"

"You, my dear, may be the break I've been waiting for for over two years."

"What?" I gasped. "I mean, you *believe* me?"

"Well, to be honest, I was about to call a psych ward until you said 'mother of macaroons.'"

"Huh? I don't get it."

"That's a code used by a bookie organization run by a guy named Bingo Bob."

"Bingo Bob!"

"You've heard of him?"

I nodded. "Yes. I think he might even be on this tape. He and Loo were planning on torching Water Loo's for the insurance money. It went up in flames this morning."

"If you actually captured that on tape, it would certainly be the icing on my racketeering case."

I shot him a worried look. "Racketeering?"

"Yes. A fancy, catch-all name for extorting money, carrying on illegal business activities, etcetera."

"Does that include cutting off fingers?"

"If dismemberment was done for extortion or monetary gain, yes. Tell me, what day did you find the finger, Ms. Fremden?"

"On my birthday. April Fool's day."

"So about three weeks ago."

"Geez, is that all?" I asked. "It seems like three *years* ago. Can you help me, then, Mr. Charles? Can you prove my innocence?"

He shrugged, but nodded hopefully. "If this tape has what I need, yes. And I'll do it pro-bono. Only fair if you've handed me my smoking gun."

"Seriously?" I said. "That's fantastic! Thank you!"

"Don't celebrate just yet, Ms. Fremden. There's still work to be done. Bingo Bob and his attorneys are slick. You had the finger and gave it to the police. How did the green dwarf know you had the finger? Unless we can show a line of evidence tracing the finger's whereabouts from Loo's knife to your couch, his lawyers could snag you as complicit. Possession is nine-tenths of the law, you know."

"Yes, I've heard that somewhere."

"I'm going to call an emergency meeting of my task force and have them listen to the tape. I'll get back with you as soon as I know anything."

"Okay. But could you answer one question for me?"

"Perhaps."

"Who's the green dwarf in the Halloween mask?"

Mr. Charles laughed.

"Oh. His name is Albert Greene. He works as a general go-for and flunkey for Bingo Bob."

"Oh."

"Ms. Fremden. Does anyone else know about this tape?"

"Just me and a few friends."

"Well, I'd encourage you to tell your friends to keep quiet about it for now. Let's keep this a secret from Bingo Bob and his defense team. Of course, we'll have to admit it as evidence in court, but if this tape has him talking about arson, the case probably won't go that far. If he has any brains, he'll plead."

"Okay. But I'm curious, Mr. Charles. If you're involved in racketeering cases, why did your office even let me make an appointment?"

"Ms. Fremden, we changed our main number twenty years ago. The only people with access to our private racketeering hotline are team members and the occasional emergency witness. Apparently, you called the magic number."

I touched the dragonfly pendant hanging around my neck and smiled.

I LEFT THE LAW OFFICES of Charles & Charles feeling like I'd just survived a week-long juice cleanse. I'd been through the wringer, but I wanted to jump and skip and float off to the moon. I turned my phone back on. There was a message from Lieutenant Jergen. I came back to earth and hit the playback button. Jergen's voice cracked over my phone.

"Ms. Fremden, the DNA results are back for the man found in the dumpster. It was not a match to the finger's DNA. I wanted you to know so you didn't worry about being up for murder charges. We're still waiting to see if Mr. Michaels is a match. I hope you have acquired legal representation by now."

Strange. Jergen had sounded almost supportive. Had the tide really, actually turned on this whole mess? Maybe Tom will have the right answers tonight when we meet, and everything will go back to normal. That wasn't too much to ask, was it?

I climbed in the old convertible and turned the ignition. All I had to do now was figure out how the finger ended up in my couch. On my windshield, a slip of green paper flapped in the breeze, held down by a wiper blade. I got out and yanked it free. It was an ad for a company promising to pay top dollar for used cars. I slid back into Maggie's bucket seat and patted the dash.

"Don't you worry, girl. I'd never trade you in."

I wadded the paper up and threw it on the floorboard. I pulled out of the parking lot and headed for home. I took a hard right and the green wad of paper rolled across the floor. *Green. Green. Where had I heard that name before?*

When I'd said 'mother of macaroons" to Hemingway, the attorney J.D. Fellows had referred to me, he'd dropped me like a hot coal. I'd figured he'd thought I was crazy. But his excuse had been *conflict of interest.* When I'd originally gone to see Fellows to get the referral, he'd sent me packing, too. Right before he did, Mr. Fellows's secretary had come over the intercom...What did she say? Mr. Greene was on the line...it was an emergency....

Was that *Mr. Greene actually Albert Greene, aka the green dwarf? Did Mr. Fellows know him? Oh my lord! If that's true, Mr. Fellows could have put the finger in my couch when he was at my party! But why would he do that?*

I was just two blocks from Fellows' office. I hung a hard right. Tom drove by in his silver 4Runner. Gorgeous Milly was in the passenger seat beside him, laughing.

Chapter Thirty-Three

Lying dirtbag! Every fiber of my being wanted to turn Maggie around and flatten those two love birds under my whitewalls. But just like Mr. Finkerman, at the moment, I had bigger fish to fry. I pulled into the parking lot of Fellows & Associates and made a quick call.

"Goober Two to Goober One."

"Goober One here."

"How's the condition of our...uh..."

"The suspect regained consciousness," Goober said. "I dropped him at his car ten minutes ago."

"You didn't mention anything to him about the tape, did you?"

"I'm not an idiot, Val."

"No, you're not. Do me a favor, don't mention the tape or any of this stuff about Loo to anyone—including Jorge."

"But—"

"I'm sorry, Goober. But I think Jorge tells Tom what we're up to all the time. I don't think Tom should be involved in this. For his career...and—"

"The burrito is in the belfry," Goober blurted over me.

"What?"

"The taco is in town."

"Goober, what the hell are you saying?"

"Good grief, woman. Jorge is here with me."

"Oh. Well, keep him out of range of Tom, okay?"

"Roger that."

"And don't tell him anything!"

"I'D LIKE TO SPEAK WITH Mr. Fellows, please," I said to the receptionist.

"Do you have an appointment?" she asked, looking down her nose at me.

I smiled sweetly. "Just tell him it's an emergency."

She stared at me blankly, her lips scrunched as if she'd just sucked on a lemon wedge.

"A *Mr. Greene* emergency," I added.

The woman whipped around and hit a button on the intercom.

"Mr. Fellows? There's a woman here about Mr. Greene. Oh. Her name?"

She looked up at me for the answer.

I crinkled my nose in a fake smile. "Why don't we just let it be a surprise."

"Uh...she says it's a surprise."

A moment later Mr. Fellows appeared wearing a grey Armani suit and a dark scowl. When he recognized me, his face brightened, then shifted to alarm.

"Val!" he shouted. "What are you doing here?"

"I need to talk to you about Mr. Greene."

Mr. Fellows tried to maintain a poker face, but was betrayed by his left eyebrow.

He nodded solemnly. "Come this way."

I followed Mr. Fellows to his office and took a seat as he hoisted his small frame into his specially made chair. He settled himself in, sighed, and looked me in the eye.

"What's your involvement with Mr. Greene?"

"As if you don't know."

MARGARET LASHLEY

Mr. Fellows looked confused. "I...I'm afraid I don't."

"Mr. Fellows, I trusted you. I came to you when I needed help—when I found that finger in my couch. You let me sit here like a moron and tell you the whole story, pretending that you didn't already know the whole spiel. How could you do that to me?"

"Val, I...I'm at a loss here."

"Are you telling me you didn't plant that finger in my couch?"

"What? Why on earth would I do that?"

"That's what I need to find out. From *you!*"

"Val, I had nothing to do with it."

"Then why did you *just now* drop everything when your receptionist said it was about Mr. Greene?"

"I...I always...my door is always open to you. You know that."

"But you didn't know it was *me.*"

Fellows hung his professional head for a moment, then looked up again as a friend.

"All right. Look, Val. Mr. Greene is my idiot nephew. He's always in some kind of shi...uh...*situation.*"

"Why didn't you tell me he was the guy who broke in my house looking for the finger?"

"Because I didn't know...until after you left. That was him on the phone when you were here last. I'm sorry for my behavior that day. He really knows how to push my buttons. I was angry."

"*You're* angry? What about me? Why didn't you tell me once you knew?"

"What was the point? The police had the finger, Albert promised not to bother you again. It seemed the easiest thing to do. He hasn't...been back to see you again, has he?"

"No. But why did you put the finger in my couch for him to come get?"

"I didn't."

"But...if *you* didn't, how in the world did the finger get in my couch? And how did your nephew know it was there?"

Fellows lined his fingertips together and knitted his brow.

"Yes. I can see your line of reasoning now. How you might come to the conclusion of my involvement. But I promise on your mother's name, Val. I didn't do it."

"Then who the hell did? And why would Albert be trying to find the finger in the first place?"

"Like I said, Val. He's an idiot. He's always getting messed up with the wrong kind of folks."

"Like 'mother of macaroons' kind of folks?"

Fellows looked me in the eye and blew out a breath.

"Precisely."

Chapter Thirty-Four

W*here do I go from here?* I was driving back home, out of ideas and almost out of hope. *Please, somebody tell me, how did that frickin' finger end up in my couch?*

I was racking my brain at a red light when a bright-yellow garage sale sign caught my eye. Of their own accord, my hands turned the steering wheel to the right, and against my will I followed the signs all the way to that purple cottage I'd stopped at a week or so ago. I pulled up in front. The plump, redheaded woman was waiting in her lawn chair in the driveway. Her money belt was around her waist, that clear-green plastic visor wrapped around her brow. She held a bag of Fritos in one hand and waved at me with the other. I waved back.

"Hey there!" she yelled. "I was hoping I'd see you again. I've got something I think you'll like."

"What is it?"

"Come see!"

I hauled my butt out of Maggie and hoofed it up the drive. The lady wiped her right hand off on the seat of her shorts. I shook her greasy hand.

"Right over here."

I followed her into her second-hand lair. The garage was stuffed to the gills with tables and bookshelves, junk heaped upon junk.

"What do you think of these?"

She reached into a box and held up three cheap figurines.

"I'll take a dollar each for 'em. Except this one. It's got a chip off the face, so it's half price."

"Sold. I'll take all three."

She eyed me curiously.

"You're an easy sale today."

"Yeah. Not much in the mood to put up a fight."

"Something knock the wind out of your sails?"

"You could say that."

"Well, I hope these little guys will cheer you up."

"I'm counting on it."

Suddenly, I felt overwhelmed by the collection of junk surrounding me.

"I gotta go. Here's three bucks. Keep the change."

I grabbed the bag of figurines and headed for Maggie. I exchanged waves with the woman as I drove away, but a deep-blue melancholy threatened to tag along for the ride. I'd lived my whole life amid someone else's leftovers. Hell, I was even a *hand-me-down baby*. That old couch had been someone's cast-off, and it had cost me plenty. I was living in my parents' house—another dream that had belonged to them, not me. I was a second-hand patsy for Finkerman. Tom had traded me in for Milly. Was I just a used-up woman ready to be thrown in the bargain bin?

I hit the gas, hoping to leave my sad thoughts in the dust. I headed toward Bimini Circle. My parent's home. I needed to pound out a few frustrations before Tom got there. Chocolate couldn't fix this. It was time for someone to die.

I LINED UP THE THREE figurines, executioner style, along the concrete block. One was a clown. Easy kill. A clown had been the inspiration for my macabre habit. I remembered my first smack-down like it was yesterday. I'd been fourteen at the time. A snotty rich girl at school had gotten my name as secret Santa. She'd known I hated clowns. Yet when it had come my turn to open my gift, inside was a clown figurine with the insipid inscription, "Waddle I do without you?" I'd loathed every molecule of its existence. After school, I'd taken it home, snuck off to the nearby vacant lot and beaten it to death with a hammer. That day, a serial ceramic killer was born.

I stared into the eyes of "Sammy the Silly Clown." Yes. He would be the first to face Val's Hammer of Injustice today. I raised my weapon above my head and let it crash down hard. The first strike was perfect. It hit at a top-down angle that cracked Sammy's hideous, smiling head in half. A few more strategic whacks and Silly Sammy had rejoined the great circus in the sky.

Next up was an angel holding a bell. Her face was already badly chipped. Her entire nose and half a cheek were missing. I figured I would be forgiven. It was a mercy killing, right? The first whack cracked her cute little haloed skull and broke off her wings. Five more blows and she was off to join the choir in heaven.

I turned my attention to the last figure. It was a blond boy with blue eyes, dressed in a cop uniform. "Petie the Police Boy" was about to be handed a death sentence. I lifted the hammer over my head. *Tom? Jergen? Nope. It was BOGO day....*

"Hey, Val!"

I glanced to my left. Laverne was at the picket fence, waving.

"Watcha doing?" she called out.

"A little housecleaning."

"Want to come over for coffee?"

I lowered my arm and placed the hammer on ground amidst the rubble of my ceramics cemetery. I picked my way through the weeds over to Laverne.

"Sorry. I don't have time. I've got to get ready for Tom's visit."

"Whew. Are you ready for the showdown?"

"I don't know. My stomach's doing belly flops. He told me the baby wasn't his, Laverne. I want to believe him, but then I saw him driving around with Milly again today. Honestly, I don't know what to think."

Laverne reached in her pocket and pulled out a small tin. She opened it up. Inside were some square, blue tablets.

"Here. Have one of these. It'll steady your nerves."

"Thanks Laverne, but I don't take drugs."

"It's herbal. Give one a try."

I picked one out of the tin and popped it in my mouth. It tasted like peppermint. Laverne closed the tin. It was a pack of breath mints.

"Laverne, that's nothing but mints."

"I know."

"How's that going to calm my nerves?"

Laverne laughed and put the tin back in her pocket.

"I give these to my dates all the time," she said. "I tell them it's Viagra."

"Does it work?"

"Let's just say this; a person believes what they want to believe."

"I believe if this keeps up much longer, my heart's going to shrivel up and die."

Laverne looked me up and down and winked.

"Well, at least your nails look fabulous."

I PACED THE FLOOR LIKE a tiger in a cage. Tom had just texted. He was on his way over. Part of me ached for him. Part of me wanted to take my hammer and finish him off, too. I'd showered, shaved and dolled myself up. I was also stone-cold sober. If this was the last time I was going to see Tom, I wanted to make it memorable.

I jumped a foot in the air when the doorbell rang. I smoothed my hair and skirt and opened the door. Tom wore jeans, a white button-down shirt and an open, serious face. He held a spring bouquet in his hand.

"These are for you, Val. Thanks for seeing me."

I took the flowers and invited him in. He followed me to the kitchen. I looked for a vase, but my mind was scrambled. I put the tea pitcher in the sink, filled it with tap water and stuck the flowers in. The awkwardness was palpable. *Screw it. I need a drink.*

"You want a drink?" I asked as I set the pitcher of daisies and lilies and bluebells on the counter.

"Yes, sure."

"Me, too. Beer or TNT?"

"It doesn't matter. Beer. It's easier."

I pulled two bottles of beer from the fridge and opened them. I handed one to Tom. He looked at it, surprised.

"Glass bottles? Fancy. What's the occasion?"

I smiled weakly at his joke, but I wasn't in the mood to laugh. I wasn't keen on getting this tragic conversation going, either. We both took a slug of beer and stared at the floor.

"Well?" I said, finally.

I looked up at Tom. His handsome face had gone serious again.

"It's a long story," he began. "Should we sit somewhere?"

"No couch."

"How about outside? Lawn chairs?"

"Okay."

I opened the sliding door to the backyard and cringed. *Crap!* Standing on the concrete block, next to the hammer, the little police boy figurine stared up at me pleadingly amidst the shattered body parts of his less-fortunate fellow captives. I walked by him to a pair of lawn chairs near the water. I hoped Tom wouldn't notice Petie in the evening twilight. We took our seats and stared out at the boats bobbing in the waterway.

"I see it's not looking too good for us cops," Tom said. "Did you grant me a stay of execution?"

I cringed again. "Yes. But it's only temporary."

"What can I say to convince you I'm a good guy?"

"I don't know. Just tell me the truth. I can live with anything but lies."

Tom took a deep breath.

"Okay. It all started around six years ago. I dated Jergen's sister Rita for a few months. She was nice, but no real sparks. Not like you and me."

Tom shot me a look that made me squirm inside.

"So, one evening, Rita and I did a double date with my best friend John. By the end of the night, his date Judy and I were on our own. To be honest, I didn't mind. It was kind of magical, the way John and Rita just hit it off like that. Like those sappy movies you girls like so much. I think it was like love at first sight for those two."

"What's that got to do with you and the baby, Tom?"

"I'm getting there. Hans—I mean *Jergen*—hated John. Let's just say, when it came to who was good enough to date his sister, Hans was a racist snob. A month or so after their first date, Rita found out she was pregnant. They wanted to get married, but knew Hans would never give them a minute's peace if they did. They came to me with this scheme. They wanted me to tell Hans that *I* got Rita pregnant but I wouldn't marry her. That way, John could step up, be the hero and make a so-called 'honest woman' out of Rita. I would take the fall. John was my best friend, so I did it. Hans fell for it. He turned his hate on me, and Rita's family accepted John."

"Geez. Are you still friends? With John?"

"No. Giving that up was part of the plan."

"What happened to the baby?"

"Miscarriage a month after they were married."

"That's terrible. I'm so sorry. But Tom, I have to ask. How do I know you're telling the truth? That the baby wasn't yours?"

"Because I wasn't sleeping with Rita. But I was afraid you wouldn't take my word for it. I had a vasectomy ten years ago. I have the records in my truck, if you want to see them."

"No. I believe you."

Tom turned and shot me a hopeful smile. "Are we good, then?"

"Is that it?"

"Yes."

Tom leaned over to kiss me. I pushed him away and stood up.

"Really, Tom? What about going through my phone? What about snooping through my papers? And what about *my* best friend Milly? I've seen you two together all over town!"

Tom shrunk back and bit his lower lip. "Crap."

"What?"

"Val, I swear. Nothing is going on between Milly and me. I know it doesn't look good, but trust me on this."

"You're kidding, right?"

"Look, she's helping me with something. I can't explain it. It's official business. An...*investigation*. It should all be over in a couple of weeks. I promise I'll tell you everything then. I swear."

Tears filled my eyes. Relief and frustration. So close, but still so far.

"I'm not good at waiting, Tom."

"I *know*. Believe me."

Tom smiled. He stood up and hugged me. His arms felt so strong. So safe. I pulled away again.

"You know what hurts the most, Tom? You weren't there when I needed you."

"I know. I wasn't there to help you, and I'm sorry. Val, I know first-hand what a nasty piece of work Jergen can be. I backed off so he would back off of you. I hope it worked."

"I guess you were right about that. I think it did help. The last message he left me...he actually sounded kind of nice."

"Good. Val, life isn't a fairytale. I can't be there for you all the time. I'm no superhero. I'm not like you, Valiant Stranger."

Tom took my chin in his hand. We locked eyes and smiled.

"I've got my weaknesses, too," I said.

"I know. Chocolate...roaches...yard sales..."

I snickered.

Tom laughed and continued, "...can't take a compliment...."

"Don't forget the worst one," I added. "Inability to smell bullcrap until it hits me in the face."

"Ah. My personal favorite."

Tom pulled me to his chest and kissed me hard on the mouth. My knees buckled. He whispered in my ear.

"I'm hoping I can add sexy cop to your list of weaknesses."

My thigh bumped against the crotch of Tom's jeans.

"Maybe I should add jealous, untrusting brunettes to yours."

Tom kissed me hard again.

"I said I was sterile, Val, not impotent. Big difference."

Big difference, indeed.

Chapter Thirty-Five

Forever was a long time to swear off something. I'd lasted about twelve minutes with booze, twelve days with men. I looked over at Tom in bed beside me. Maybe fate hadn't given us the finger after all.

A week had passed since I'd smashed any figurines. Petie the Police Boy had gotten his last-minute stay of execution. The tension between Tom and I had slacked off, but wasn't totally erased. He still had a week before he had to spill his guts about Milly.

Milly and I were talking again, too. It was a tenuous time for me. I tried my best to find a way back to our old routine, but it was a struggle, given my lingering feelings of mistrust. On top of all that, I had to dodge Finkerman's calls while I waited for the DNA results to come in on the finger. I was cleaning up breakfast dishes the morning after a very nice Taco Tuesday when the phone rang. My attorney, Bernard Charles, was on the other end of the line.

"Ms. Fremden?"

"Yes. Hello, Mr. Charles."

"We've analyzed the tape. Good and bad news. Good news, you got Loo and Meyers on tape plotting the arson."

"Meyers?"

"Bingo Bob."

"Oh. Right. That's good for your case, right?"

"Yes and no. The fire investigation report came back. They can't prove arson. Looks like either they covered their tracks well or faulty wiring beat them to it. The place burned down due to a grease fire. Can you believe that?"

"Yes. I was in the back kitchen once. I'm scarred for life."

"Bad luck all around."

"Where do you go from here?"

"We've got other angles to pursue."

"What about Loo's confession? Cutting off Mickie's finger?"

"Well, your tactics were dubious at best, Ms. Fremden. But I promise I'll do all I can to get you off. You won't be facing direct charges. The only charge that has a chance of sticking at this point is conspiracy. Unless, that is, you've figured out the connection. How the finger ended up with you."

"No. Nothing yet. Could I get a copy of the tape?"

"Certainly. I'll leave one at reception for you. Hopefully, with any luck, DNA will prove the finger wasn't even Mr. Michaels."

"Really? Do you get a lot of missing fingers in your line of work?"

"You'd be surprised."

I hung up and padded over to my computer and googled the news. "No Evidence of Arson in Local Restaurant Fire." *Some people have all the luck.* I'd just stuck my hands in the dishwater again when my phone rang. It was Finkerman.

"Ms. Fremden, your 'bigger fish' just slipped off the hook."

Nope. This was definitely not turning out to be my lucky day.

"What do you want, Finkerman?"

"Why, your money, of course. Don't be silly."

"Silly?"

"Hey, it's nothing personal. But a million dollars just went up in smoke. I've got a client here says you cut his finger off. You had the finger. You're low-hanging fruit."

I hate you! You disgusting excuse for a human being! I took a deep breath and swallowed my anger. "Okay. How much do you want?"

"Ah. The voice of reason at last. Twenty-thousand ought to do it."

"But that's twice what you—"

"That's the price of adding on a wild, million-dollar goose chase, Ms. Fremden."

"Okay. But I want to do this face-to-face."

"My pleasure. When and where?"

"Water Loo's parking lot. Two o'clock."

"I'll be there with the paperwork. Don't forget your checkbook."

"I won't." *And I won't forget to bring my recording of Loo's confession, either. I can't wait to see the look on your smarmy face when your last fish jumps out of the fryer.*

I SQUEEZED THE LAST drop of Ty D Bol into the toilet. I flushed and watched it swirl away. Hopefully the recording would be enough to rid me of Finkerman. My house chores were done. It was time for my reward. I slipped on a sundress, inched into some sandals and headed to the drugstore on 107th. I was in desperate need of Ty D Bol and chocolate.

I was standing at the checkout with a Mounds bar and a family-sized bottle of my favorite toilet cleaner when I saw Pops walk in, grinning from ear to ear.

"Hey, Pops!"

"Val! How's my girl?"

"She's running great, as always."

"No, I meant *you*."

"Doing okay. Hoping to finish off some business this afternoon. You're all smiles today, Pops."

"I finished off some business myself. Sold me a car. Remember that gold Cadillac? The one that crazy woman put five-hundred down on?"

"Yeah."

"She and her boyfriend came by this morning. Bought the Caddy full price. I told her I couldn't give her that deposit back, being as she was late and all. She didn't bat an eyelash. Said she'd always wanted her a gold Cadillac, and she was gonna have it no matter what."

"Hey, good for you!"

"Yeah. You know, Val, normally, you can't trust a crow-eyed woman. But this time she up and proved me wrong. Whipped out a wad of hunnert-dollar bills and peeled sixty of 'em off right into my hand. Didn't even make a dent in that roll of hers."

"Wow. Where'd she get that kind of money?"

"Said they just won a million dollars. The man with her opened up a duffle bag and flashed me a wad of cash that could choke a wood chipper. Said they was gonna live like a king and queen down in Mexico. I wished 'em well and they drove that Caddy right off the lot. Gonna miss her. She was a beauty."

"Yeah. She sure was."

I DROVE TOWARD THE law offices of Charles & Charles with a mouth full of Mounds and a mindful of angst. Should I tell Mr. Charles what I'd just heard? What if the people who bought Pops' Cadillac really *were* lottery winners and weren't Loo and Latrina? I'd have made a fool of myself. *But what if they were!*

I parked Maggie sideways in the empty parking lot at Charles's office. The door was locked. I banged on it and a small, brown envelope fell out of the mailbox slot. It had my name on it. I tore it open. The recorder was inside. I slipped it into my pocket and leaned over a window and peeked inside. The place was empty. Not a stick of furniture or a piece of paper on the floor. Nothing.

I called Mr. Charles's number. No answer. What was going on here? I left a message for him to call me and glanced at the time on my phone. It was 1:30 p.m.

I didn't have enough time to go home, change clothes and get back to Water Loo's by two o'clock, so I took a slow tour down Gulf Boulevard and parked in the empty lot that used to surround the restaurant. A man was there, walking around with a tape measure and a clipboard.

"What are you doing?" I asked.

"Lot measurements. I'm a property appraiser. You interested in buying the lot?"

"Maybe. What's it going for?"

"Hard to say. Somewhere between quarter and half a mill, it being on Gulf, you know."

"Yeah. Location, location, location."

"Exactly. Well, I'm all done here. Should be on the market in a few days. Crown Royalty Group, if you're interested."

"Thanks. I'll keep it in mind."

The man drove off. I thought about all the times I'd been in Water Loo's with the gang. Now the place was erased as if it never existed. A few minutes later, a huge, lemon-yellow Hummer pulled up. A tinted window zipped down, revealing the frizzy-haired head of Ferrol Finkerman.

"Geez, woman. Get in my vehicle. It's too hot to sit outside."

I got out, walked to the passenger side of the hummer and pulled open the door. Inside, Finkerman had a laptop desk set up in the console between two swiveling seats as big as living-room lounge chairs.

"Geez. This thing is bigger than my old apartment."

"Lap of luxury is the way I roll, Ms. Fremden. Here's the agreement."

Finkerman handed me a stack of papers.

"This looks pretty complicated."

"It's all routine stuff. Standard contract. Here. Use my lucky pen. You have your checkbook?"

I took the pen. It was lemon-yellow like his Hummer, with a round smiley-face head on top. I thought about jamming it in his eye, but settled on a sweeter kind of revenge.

"I didn't bring the checkbook. I have something better. Listen."

I hit play on the recorder. Finkerman's smugness disappeared like July snow as he listened to loopy Loo slur out his confession under the influence of Jack Daniels. Suddenly, he smiled and reached out a hand for me to shake.

"Well played, Ms. Fremden. I'm back on track with Loo and his million. My client will be pleased."

"So I'm off the hook?"

"Not exactly. As I recall, you still had possession of the finger."

"Not if it turns out to be someone else's finger instead of Mickie's."

"True. But you and I both know it most likely belongs to him."

I grabbed the recorder and stuck it in my bra.

"If you don't let me off, Finkerman, you don't get the tape."

"Don't need it. I've got my own copy, now."

Finkerman patted his pocket. I picked up the yellow pen. A gold Cadillac pulled up in the lot, saving me from assault charges. I stared and pointed out the windshield.

"There's your real money, Finkerman."

We watched from the tinted windows as Loo got out, walked over to the spot where Water Loo's front door used to be, and took a piss. Latrina climbed out and recorded it on her phone.

"Look at them. Disgraceful," Finkerman said.

"*They're* disgraceful?"

"Look, someone has to do my job. I'm just looking out for the little guy."

"How little is it?"

I patted my groin. Finkerman stared at me blankly for a second, then laughed out loud.

"You're clever. I like you. Tell me why I should drop this nuisance case against you. I'm in a good mood. I might just listen."

"What if I told you that those two people over there are Water Loo's owners Loo and Latrina stopping to take souvenir photos?"

"What?"

"They cashed in their insurance settlement. Got the money in a duffle bag in their car. They're heading to Mexico."

Loo and Latrina got back in the gold Cadillac and pulled out onto Gulf Boulevard.

"What? Are you serious? We can't let them get away!"

Finkerman shifted the Hummer into drive and took off after the Cadillac.

"What are you doing?" I yelled at him.

"I don't know. I'll think of something."

"Let me out!"

"Nope. No time."

The Cadillac turned right on First Avenue South. Finkerman followed suit.

"They must be heading for the interstate. Can't let that happen."

"You're crazy, Finkerman. Pull over and let me out!"

"Shut up, I'm trying to think, here!"

Finkerman hit the gas. The Caddy turned left, then right again onto Central Avenue

"Have you lost your mind? What are you planning on doing?"

"I'm not losing that million. They have to pull over sometime. I...I've got sedatives. I could drug them. Take the money. Help me out, Fremden, and you're off the hook. I won't bother you again."

"Are you insane?"

The gold Cadillac pulled off Central up to the Taco Bus restaurant. Loo and Latrina climbed out.

"Perfect," Finkerman said. "Here's the plan. You distract them, I'll slip in the sedatives."

"Then what?"

"I'll grab their keys, then the money. They'll wake up later all 'Boo-hoo. Money gone.' Couldn't happen to a nicer couple."

Finkerman parked the Hummer and pulled out a bottle of pills.

"Are you in?"

I glanced around and nodded.

Finkerman unlocked the doors. I jumped out, ran into the street and flagged down the police car I'd spotted a block behind us. He turned on his lights and stopped in the middle of Central. I ran to his window.

"Help! I was being held against my will by that man!"

I pointed at Finkerman. He made a run for his vehicle. The cop pulled his cruiser up in front of the Hummer, blocking his escape. Finkerman looked at the cop and wilted like lettuce on a patty melt.

"Crap."

"Mr. Finkerman, we meet again," the cop said. "You know the drill."

Finkerman leaned up against the Hummer and put his hands behind his back. The cop cuffed him and turned to me.

"And who are you?"

"Val Fremden. Officer, this man was trying to kidnap me and steal those people's money."

"Not surprising. Finkerman, I'm going to have to bring you in for questioning."

Finkerman sneered at me as he was led to the police car.

"It's only he said, she said," he yelled. "I'll be home in time for supper."

I patted my boob.

"I don't think so, Finkerman. I've got it all on tape."

Chapter Thirty-Six

A lot happened over the next week. On Tuesday, I worked out a deal with Finkerman. I dropped the charges of kidnapping and false imprisonment, and he dropped his nuisance lawsuit against me. I was finally free of the fickle finger of fate, even though I didn't know how or why it had pointed at me. On Wednesday, my attorney, Bernard Charles, finally returned my call. He apologized for the delay, and explained that his offices had to relocate suddenly. He couldn't tell me why, but he did let me know his team was still on the case of Bingo Bob. He told me to keep his number, in case I ever needed it.

Finkerman called on Friday to tell me Loo and Latrina had settled out of court with him on Mickie's behalf for an undisclosed sum. Their vacant lot on Gulf Boulevard sold the same day it was listed. Finkerman also said Loo and Latrina told him they were moving to The Villages in Ocala. I hoped they did—before they lost whatever they had left at the dog track.

As for the rest of us, we stayed put in sunny St. Petersburg. We hadn't settled on a new hangout yet, but a picnic table in the soft sand at Caddy's on Sunset Beach would do for now.

"Heard yore off the hook for false infingerment," Winky said, then tipped his head back to let in some beer.

"I'm gonna miss Water Loo's," Jorge sighed.

I grimaced. "You all know they 'recycled' the coffee there, don't you?"

"Never did nobody no harm, Val," Winky said.

"Are you sure?"

Goober tipped his baseball cap at me and smiled.

"With this crowd, it'd be hard to spot true brain damage."

"Hey, speak for yourself, com-pardre," Winky shot back.

"Jorge, I'm curious," I said. "What are you going to miss about that place? It was a dump."

"Yeah. But it was *our* dump."

I sighed. "True enough."

"I'm gonna miss the rag box," Winky said. "I enjoyed partakin' of the recycled clothing amenities."

"You're the *only* one," I said. "I never saw anyone else go near that mangy box."

"Sure they did. All the time."

"Yeah. Right."

"Okay, Miss Smarty Pants. I remember one. 'Bout a month ago. This feller was going through the rag box and picked out that old jacket Winnie made me wear to your party. I warned him it was itchy as a chigger bite. He took my advice and put it back. I remember he was a real sociable feller. Even asked about your party. When I told him I'd fixed your air conditioner, he told me his was busted too. Poor feller couldn't find no reliable, honest repair man. Asked if I'd do it. All he needed was a reference. So I give him your name and number."

"Oh yeah," I said. "I remember you talking about him before. He never called. What was his name?"

"Not good with names, Val. But I remember he was a funny little fella. What'n no more than four feet tall, tops. I was kinda surprised he wanted to hire me. The way he'd gone through the pockets on that jacket, you'd think he didn't have a dime to his name."

Chapter Thirty-Seven

Saturday morning, I woke with a nasty hangover. But it had been worth it. The last piece of the puzzle had fallen out of Winky's mouth last night, and I'd celebrated with drinks all around.

Loo must have cut Mickie's finger off to pay a debt to Bingo Bob—either his or Mickie's. Loo stuck the finger in the jacket pocket for Bingo Bob to pick up, figuring nobody would go near the rag box. Unbeknownst to Winky, he'd brought the finger along with him when he'd worn the jacket to my party. He told me last night that he'd taken the jacket off and laid it on top of the couch when he'd helped Tom move the ratty old thing into my place. The finger must have fallen out of the pocket in transit, and gotten wedged between the cushions.

The way I saw it, the day after my party Bingo Bob must have sent Green Dwarf to get the finger from the jacket. By then, Winky had already put it back in the box, minus the finger. It was Winky's big mouth that had led Albert Greene right to my place. But I couldn't complain. It was Winky's love of Easter eggs that had made it all good again.

I settled back into bed with an Advil and a cappuccino. I didn't even bother to google the news. I was just about to doze off again when my phone rang.

"Yeah?"

"Val? Is that you?"

I cleared my groggy throat. "Yeah. Hi Milly."

"Hey yourself. I've been trying to get ahold of you for two weeks. Would you like to go to Safety Harbor Spa with me today? I know it's last minute. But I've got free passes and they expire tomorrow."

"Free passes?"

"Yeah. The works...for two. Massages, facials, pedicures. Are you in?"

Tom still hadn't explained what was going on with him and Milly. But he'd told me last night that I had to trust him for just a few more days. I liked Milly. I didn't want to let her go. I'd lost so many friends already. I decided to take a chance. I hoped she would turn out to be worth the risk.

"Uh...okay. Sure, Milly. What time shou—"

"Great! I'll pick you up in ten minutes."

"Geez. That's barely enough time to shave my legs!"

"Are you complaining?"

"No."

"Good. I declare this is a crab-free day."

I laughed. "Okay. Fair enough."

I clicked off the phone and jumped in the shower. I only needed four minutes to shave, but it took me five minutes to decide which panties to wear. With massages, it was a tricky subject. *Too sexy* panties and I'd send the wrong message to the masseuse. *Too matronly* panties and I'd send the wrong message to myself.

I was inching into my shoes when the doorbell rang. I opened the door to find Milly shifting from one foot to the other like she needed to pee.

"Come on! Let's go!" She reached out and tugged on my arm.

"Hold on! Don't you want to see the place? You've never even been here before."

"I will when we get back. We gotta go! I made massage appointments for nine."

"That's like *thirty minutes* from now."

"*Exactly.* Come on!"

I locked the door behind me and jumped in the passenger seat of Milly's red Beemer. It was just the opposite of Shabby Maggie. The BMW was shiny, new, and had all the latest modern gadgets—like power steering, power brakes and a CD player. I tried to hide my envy from Maggie as we peeled out of the driveway and left her behind in the dust.

"How can you afford this thing, Milly? It's got more controls than a space shuttle."

"I work at an accounting office, remember? When you're in charge of the numbers, you're *in charge of the numbers.*"

"Don't say another word. My boyfriend's a cop, remember."

"Yes, I know."

"What's *that* supposed to mean?"

"What's *what* supposed to mean?"

I studied Milly's body language. She was too perky. And she looked nervous, like she'd been caught in a lie. *Was she having an affair with Tom? Or was I just the most paranoid idiot on the planet?*

Milly maneuvered her BMW down US 19 like a race car driver on crack. The tires squealed when she took the exit toward Safety Harbor. I had to hang onto the door handle to keep from toppling over. As we sped across the Bayside Bridge, I tried to keep my eyes on the scenery and my trap shut, but sometimes my mouth had a mind of its own.

"Milly, do you think it's okay to go through someone's phone...when you're in a relationship, I mean?"

"Hell no! There ought to be a law against it!"

She glanced over at me, then backpedaled.

"I mean, unless you did already. Then it's okay."

I was glad for Milly's support, but it wasn't like her to back down like that. Did she do it out of friendship? Guilt? Pity?

"No, I didn't go through anyone's phone. I just saw someone do it on TV."

"Oh. In that case, it's *definitely* a big no-no in my book."

Milly was either a good friend or a good liar. For the moment, I decided to give her the benefit of a doubt.

MILLY AND I SAT IN a small, dimly lit reception room with two other women, wearing nothing but thick, white-cotton robes and whichever panties we had fated ourselves to. The door opened and a short, unattractive man with curly hair and a big split nose came in. He was dressed in a white polo shirt, white shorts, white socks and black tennis shoes.

"Valerie?" he asked, and looked around the room.

"That's me," said the woman to my right.

"This way, please."

The woman got up and left with him. Milly and I rolled our eyes at each other like schoolgirls. The door cracked open again. A fat woman of around fifty with a butch haircut peeked in. She looked as out of place in her white dress as a pig in a ball gown.

"Teresa?"

The woman next to Milly blew out a breath. "That's me."

She disappeared with the woman in white, leaving Milly and me alone.

"Milly, did you tell them you wanted a male masseuse?"

"No. I just took the luck of the draw."

We both grimaced as the door cracked open again. In stepped a guy too gorgeous to be anything but gay. His jet-black hair was slicked back into a neat curl behind his ear. Trendy stubble darkened his square jaw, and his tan, buff arms rippled with muscles. Milly and I both held our breath.

"Val?"

I smirked. Milly scowled.

"Um. That would be *me*. Bye, Milly!"

As I sashayed out the door with my hunky man-masseuse, I was glad I'd opted for my sexy panties. I followed him down the hall like a lost fawn.

"Here we are," he said. He opened the door to a small room glowing with scented candles and humming with soft, relaxing music.

"I'm Kevin. Undress to your comfort level and lie down on your stomach. I'll be back in a minute to check on you."

He winked a dark-brown eye at me and I suddenly needed to pee. After he left, I peeked out the door. Down the hallway on the right, I saw a restroom sign. I scampered to the toilet, pulled down my tiny, tiger-striped panties and squatted over the bowl. I emptied my bladder and reached for the roll. It was empty.

"No! This can't be happening!" I said aloud.

My thighs began to wobble from hovering over the toilet.

What now? I put my hands on my thighs to brace them, and heard a crinkling sound. *Paper! In my robe pocket!* I reached in and pulled out a handful of wrinkly coupons and advertisements. *Better than nothing.* I wiped myself as best I could with them and flushed them down the toilet. I pulled up my panties, scurried back to my room, flung off my robe and dove, face-down on the massage bed. The sheet was still settling down on my derriere when Kevin knocked on the door.

"Ready for me?" he asked.

"Yes."

"Good!" Kevin entered and closed the door behind him.

"I'll start with your legs," he whispered.

"Okay."

Kevin ran his warm, strong fingers along my right calf. I bit my lip. His hand moved up past my knee to my lower thigh. As he massaged my hamstrings, I closed my eyes. He moved the sheet up higher, all the way to my panties.

His hand stopped suddenly. I felt a slight tug on my thigh. Kevin *started to snicker.*

My eyes flew open. I bolted upright, red-faced, and pulled the sheet around me.

"Is my butt really that funny, Kevin?"

"No! I'm sorry! It's just that..." Kevin buckled and burst into laughter again. "I'm sorry. It's just...I never got a tip like this before. Here. This was on your thigh."

Kevin reached toward me. Between his elegant finger and thumb was a dollar-off coupon for Anusol hemorrhoid salve.

I WAS PROBABLY THE only woman on earth who ever wanted to leave a day spa early. I didn't mention a word about my coupon catastrophe to Milly. I let her think the special looks I got from Kevin during our side-by-side pedicures had nothing to do with discounts on itchy-ass crème.

"Do you want to do the sauna next?" Milly asked, eyeing me jealously. "Or are you hot and bothered enough?"

I looked at the ox of a woman filing callouses off Milly's heels. A foot away, handsome Kevin was busy massaging oil onto my toes. The touch of his hands made me squirm. Not from delight, but embarrassment. I didn't dare make eye contact with him. I put on a brave façade.

"Sour grapes, Milly. Sour grapes."

Milly stared at Kevin. "Yeah. Li'l bit."

"After this, let's leave, Milly. I'm starving."

"But I hear they make a great spa lunch here, Val. And we can stay and eat in our robes."

"Yeah. I'm not in the mood for grass clippings on cardboard."

"Are you sure? It's included."

"Milly, sometimes coupons aren't worth using."

Kevin stifled a laugh. His hand jerked and he painted a stripe of red nail polish across my big toe. Milly eyed me with suspicion, but said nothing.

MILLY AND I WERE STANDING beside her Beemer in the spa parking lot. I wanted to go home.

"Val, it's only two o'clock. Let's go shopping. Have a drink somewhere." She shot me an envious look. "Maybe you can ask *Kevin* to join us."

"Milly, like I said, he's gay. I just want to go home."

"Oh! Look at all the shops! Come on. I'll buy you lunch."

My traitorous stomach gurgled. "Okay. Then we're going home."

We walked along Safety Harbor's quaint old main street. Between a seafood restaurant and a guitar-picking barber shop was a boutique selling the kind of tacky, nautical tourist crap visitors to Florida found oddly irresistible. A sign in the window read, "Starfish Wishes and Mermaid Dreams." Milly pointed at it and scowled.

"Makes me want to bust a cap in a barnacle's butt."

I grinned. "How about this place? Raw oysters. Eight bucks a dozen. Not bad."

"Anything but oysters, please!"

"I thought you loved them, Milly."

"I do. Or let's just say I did. I'm still recovering from a bad date last night."

"What's that got to do with oysters?"

"Let's order a drink and I'll give you all the gory details."

A waitress led us to a table by a window and took our order. Milly looked over at me.

"Two margaritas and two fried shrimp baskets?" she asked.

"That'll work."

The waitress wrote down our order and left. Milly turned and gave me the lowdown.

"Okay. I met this guy on MatchMate. He said he was five-foot eight. So I thought I'd give him a break and wear flats. I meet him at

PJ's Oyster Bar last night. No heels and he's still eyeballs to boobs with me. He couldn't have been more than five-foot two. There ought to be a law against lying about your height. I mean, did he think I wouldn't notice?"

"He can't help that he's short."

"I get that. But he can help lying about it."

"True enough."

"He was bald, too. Before you go judging me, Val, I know he had no control over that either. But he *could* help the fact that he wore Birkenstocks, a ridiculous Hawaiian print shirt and a baseball cap. What hair he had left was tied in a greasy ponytail. It hung down his back like the tail of a drowned rodent."

"Eww. The rat tail. That's the worst!"

"Oh no. The worst is yet to come. When we sat down to dinner, the first thing this guy asked me was whether I was going to have one glass of wine or two, because it was cheaper to order by the bottle than by the glass."

"How quaint."

"I told him I'd have just one glass. He ordered that, along with a dozen raw oysters for us to share. If he thought it was going to be an aphrodisiac, he should have asked me first. I could have saved him even more money."

"Nice."

"You won't believe this part. He counted the oysters, then divided them on the plate so we both got six each."

I shrugged. "Eh."

"After I'd eaten my six, he took his tiny seafood fork and went to work on the meat left on the shells. Val, he was so caught up in getting every last morsel that I could have been all the way home before he noticed I'd left!"

"Geez!"

"*Then* came the *piece de résistance*. When he was finally done picking over the oysters, he used that same little fork to *pick his teeth* for—I dunno—five minutes? I ordered another glass of wine. It was worth it just to watch him wince. When the check came, I insisted on splitting it. I wanted to make sure he didn't feel like I 'owed' him anything. I handed him my half in cash and said I had to go. I wasn't lying, either. If I'd stayed another second I'd have kicked my own self in the butt."

"That sounds pretty crappy. But at least he didn't take you for all you were worth."

Milly's angry, sneering face melted.

"No. You're right. Just thirty bucks."

"So count yourself lucky."

"Your German guy, Val. How much did he cost?"

"Monetarily? Eh. Just everything."

"That's horrible! I'm sorry."

"It wasn't a total loss. I figure if I can survive him, I can survive anything. Puts silly things like your date into perspective, you know?"

"Are you saying I should have given this guy more credit?"

"Hell no! If he'd lie about his height, he'd lie about anything. I guess I'm just saying that the guy isn't worth getting all worked up over. Thirty bucks? Small change. By tomorrow he should be nothing but a stupid, distant memory."

"Like your Germany guy?"

"Friedrich? No. If the going rate is thirty bucks a day, I'll still be thinking about him into the next millennium."

IT WAS NEARLY FIVE o'clock by the time Milly and I finished eating lunch and window shopping the entire Main Street of Safety Harbor. The sun hung low in the sky, but Milly's manic need for speed this morning had mellowed considerably. It was nearly six when Milly hooked a left off Gulf Boulevard into Bahia Shores.

As she turned onto Bimini Circle, I saw Tom's silver 4Runner parked in my drive.

"What's he doing here?" I asked.

"I thought you two lived together."

"Well, not exactly."

Milly pulled her BMW up behind Tom's 4Runner and cut the engine.

"I'll take that tour of your place now, if you don't mind."

Did she really want to see my place, or did she want to see Tom?

"I'm kind of tired. How about another time?"

"Come on, Val, there's no time like the present."

Crap. I guess I had no choice.

Chapter Thirty-Eight

I opened my front door and nearly fell over.

"Surprise!"

A pile of familiar faces grinned back at me. Winky. Winnie. Laverne. Goober. Jorge. And Tom.

"What's going on?" I asked.

"Welcome to your *proper* birthday party," Tom said.

He slapped a sparkly plastic tiara on my head. I adjusted my crown and looked around my place. Peeking out from behind my friends, colored balloons floated toward the ceiling, tied to every chair, picture and lamp. A huge cake lay on the kitchen counter, covered in a forest of candles. A ton of food and drinks surrounded it.

"Wow! This is too much!"

"There's more," Laverne said and pointed to her left. "Look."

I followed the line of her manicured finger. My mouth fell open. My new sofa sat against the wall. I could barely make it out for all the gifts heaped upon it.

"My couch!"

"It got here today," Laverne said. "I threatened them with the wrath of a Vegas showgirl if they didn't deliver it before four today."

"Looks like it worked," I said.

"Ready for a TNT?" Winnie asked.

"Sure, thanks!"

I turned to Milly. "You knew."

"Of course. We've been planning this for weeks."

"Oh." Tears filled my eyes. I hugged Milly. "Thanks," I whispered in her ear.

"You're welcome. I got you a gift, too, girlfriend."

"Really? What is it?"

"Let's just say I won't be the only one riding into the sunset on a Pleasure Pony."

I laughed out loud. Winky, Jorge, Goober and Laverne came up to me carrying a beautiful pink-foiled gift bag.

"Happy birthday, Val! We all chipped in for these."

I took the bag. "It's so pretty! I like the little pink fl—"

"Just open it, gaul-dang it!" Winky hollered.

I shot the freckle-faced redneck a mock scowl."Okay, hold your horses!"

I pushed aside the tissue paper. Inside were a jumble of figurines. I blushed. "Ha ha. Very funny."

"Let's see 'em," Winky said.

They all grinned at me like a pride of Cheshire cats. I pulled the figures out one by one and stood them on the counter next to the cake. A slender, red-headed ballerina. A black-haired girl with glasses. A cocoa-skinned boy. A freckled kid in overalls. A bald shoemaker with a big moustache. A blonde girl with a shopping bag. When I unwrapped Petie the Police Boy, I finally realized the trinkets were meant to represent each of my friends. But there was still one in the bag. I pulled it out. It was a brunette with a saw and a hammer. I smiled up at them wryly.

"I take it I'm Sassy Sallie."

"Woo hoo!" Winky hollered.

"Right on the money," Goober said.

"Took us a month of yard sale-ing, but we finally found what we were looking for," Laverne said.

"Well, they're...amazing. Thank you all."

"Now I need to show you something," Tom said. "Here, put on this blindfold."

"You can't show me something when I'm blindfolded," I argued. "Besides, someone already tried to kidnap me once this month."

"Ha ha. We're not taking you anywhere. Just put it on."

I slipped the mask over my eyes. I felt Tom's strong hand take mine and lead me across the living room. I heard the sliding glass door move and warm air hit my face. Tom led me outside and took off my mask. My jaw dropped to my chest.

My former trash-heaped, weed-infested yard had been transformed into a tropical oasis. A stone walkway wove a path through freshly laid grass to a swing by the water with a canopy top. A hammock hung between two palm trees. And in one corner, a thatch-roofed tiki bar was lit up with Christmas lights. Mr. Fellows was behind the counter. He waved at me and raised his margarita glass.

"Do you like it?" Tom asked, and wrapped his arms around me.

"I love it."

He took my chin softly in his hand and looked me in the eyes.

"Good. Because I love *you*, Val."

Oh my lord! Tom had never said the 'L' word to me before! But...I wasn't ready to say it back. I'd made a promise I'd never again force myself to say or be something I wasn't. I had to keep my word to myself, or I'd be lost...*again.*

"I...I don't know what to say, Tom."

Tom smiled at me tenderly and kissed my nose.

"It's okay. 'Thank you' will do for now."

Chapter Thirty-Nine

After Laverne hobbled home in her high heels and the squeaky old Dodge full of party guests left, I fixed another TNT. I sat at a barstool and studied the funny figurines lined up on the kitchen counter as Tom finished up the dishes.

"So this is my new circle of friends," I said.

Tom glanced up at me and smiled. "Looks like."

"They really do look like everyone. Especially yours, Petie the Police Boy."

Tom laughed. "I think Sassy Sallie has you pegged, too."

"Ha ha. You know, we'll have to find one for Mr. Fellows."

"I'm sure he'd appreciate that."

I picked up Sassy Sally and Petie the Police Boy. I glanced over at Tom to make sure he wasn't watching, and made the two kiss. I smiled to myself and carried them to the mantle. They and the other figurines were going to take pride of place next to Glad in her piggybank.

As I reached up to put the figurines on the mantle, I realized that Glad wasn't there. *Where had I seen her last? Oh yeah.* I wandered out into the beautiful, tropical backyard, then came back into the house.

"Tom, where's my mom's RV?"

Tom looked up from the dishes.

"Oh. I sold it. To a scrapper. He hauled it away this morning."

"No!"

"Val, it was just a piece of junk."

"Tom, you don't understand. My mother was in there!"

DEAR READER,

Thanks so much for continuing on with Two Crazy! I hope you enjoyed the story. Val is the universe's favorite victim of circumstance. The idea of the fickle finger of fate seemed like a natural foil. Val has landed on her feet, but things never go totally smoothly for her.

In Two Crazy, I wanted Val to have to rely on others for a change, even when things seem totally out of control. Letting go is a big issue for many of us. Here, Val sees what it's like to have her character come under suspect—and even her sanity! Lol! It helps her begin to forge relationships and bonds beyond her old comfort zone.

If you'd like to know when my future novels come out, please subscribe to my newsletter. I won't sell your name or send too many notices to your inbox.

Newletter Link: https://dl.bookfunnel.com/fuw7rbfx21

Thanks again for reading my book! Sometimes life really can be a bit Two Crazy. ;)

Sincerely,

Margaret Lashley

P.S. If you'd like to check out the next book in the series, Three Dumb, I've included a sample for you in the back of this book. Or click here and read the Look Inside:

https://www.amazon.com/dp/B074W8VBFN

P.S.S. I live for reviews! The link to leave yours is right here:

https://www.amazon.com/dp/B071KYVB8X#customerReviews

P.S.S.S. (Sounds like something a snake would say!) If you'd like to contact me, you can reach me by:

Website: https://www.margaretlashley.com

Email: contact@margaretlashley.com

Facebook: https://www.facebook.com/valandpalspage/

What's Next for Val?

I hope you enjoyed *Two Crazy: Bust a Move. Click the link below now and leave a review. I read every single one!*
https://www.amazon.com/dp/B071KYVB8X#customerReviews
Thank you so much! You rock!
Don't miss another new release! Follow me on Amazon and BookBub and you'll be notified of every new crazy Val adventure.
Follow me on Amazon:
https://www.amazon.com/-/e/B06XKJ3YD8
Follow me on BookBub:
https://www.bookbub.com/search/authors?search=Margaret%20Lashley

Ready for more Val?

Where does Val go from here? Will she find the RV and rescue Glad before the old Minnie Winnie ends up crushed and thrown on the scrap heap?
Enjoy the following excerpt from the next Val Fremden Mystery:

Three Dumb!

Three Dumb—a Peek Inside Val's Next Adventure!

Chapter One:

"**H**ow could you do it, Tom?"

I stared into the sea-green eyes of Lieutenant Thomas Foreman, my cop boyfriend. He was in the kitchen drying dishes, as happy as a clam on Prozac. He'd just pulled off a surprise 49th birthday party for me right under my nose, and was swaggering in self-pride about it.

The festivities had ended just a moment ago, when Laverne, my next-door neighbor and former Vegas showgirl, finally took the hint and wobbled back over to her place on those stork legs of hers. It hadn't been easy to convince her it was time to go. I'd had to change into my pajamas, tidy the couch cushions around her, take the wineglass from her hand, and, when all that failed, I'd resorted to yawning in her face. Laverne never was one for subtlety.

Tom raised a blond eyebrow on his smug, unforgivably handsome face. "Val, with you on my case, keeping it under wraps was no piece of cake."

He winked and grabbed a glass from the kitchen drain board. His lip curled into a satisfied smile as he wiped the glass dry with a dishcloth, oblivious to my growing rage. I crossed my arms and planted my feet. My mind was made up. I had a right to be pissed, and no one was going to take that away from me.

"I would hope not, Tom," I hissed, "as it probably involved forgery on your part."

Tom blanched and looked up, surprised at my anger. "Wait a second. You're not talking about *the party?*"

"No! I'm talking about selling my mother's RV—*without even asking me!*"

"Oh...*that.*"

Tom grinned at his own cleverness. He obviously didn't realize how close he was to being strangled to death with that dang dishtowel.

"Well, that *was* the tricky part, Val. And you almost caught me. I had to rifle through your silly shoebox filing system to find the title to it. It was still registered in Glad's name, but I signed it over. Seeing as she's dead, I didn't think she'd mind."

"Arrgh! Tom, I didn't mean how did you do it *logistically*. I meant how could you do it *at all?* The Minnie Winnie was *mine*. My mother's. It was...."

Tom dropped the cloth on the counter and folded his arms over his chest, mirroring mine.

"It was a piece of junk, Val. I traded it for the tiki hut. I don't know why you're so angry. I think you got the better half of the deal."

I raised my hands in frustration. "You still don't get it. It was *all I had left* of Glad—besides the piggybank with her ashes. And Tom, the piggybank was *inside the RV*."

Tom's face drooped. His arms fell limp to his sides. "Oh. I...I didn't know."

"Well, now you *do*. Why couldn't you have just asked me first?"

Tom bit his lower lip and scrunched his nose. "I don't know. It sounds lame *now*, Val. But it would have spoiled the surprise."

"And *avoided* this one."

Hot, angry tears rimmed my eyes. Tom winced sympathetically and put his arms around me.

"I'm sorry, Val. But how in the world did Glad's piggybank end up in the RV anyhow?"

I thought back to the drunken night a week and a half ago, when my imagination and half a bottle of gin had convinced me that Tom and my best friend Milly were having an affair. I'd spent a lost night in the old RV, commiserating with my mother's spirit as she'd stared back at me, wise and all-knowing, through a plastic, holographic monocle....

My face flushed. I jerked away from Tom's arms.

"Look. I don't have to explain myself to you, Tom. What I *need now* is to know where I can find the RV and get Glad back."

Tom took a step backward and showed me his open palms. "Okay! Take it easy! A buddy at work gave me the name of a junk dealer out in Pinellas Park. I've got his card around here somewhere."

Tom's eyes scanned the kitchen counter for the card, then his face registered a thought. He reached toward his right butt cheek and pulled his wallet out of the back pocket of his jeans.

"Tom, I know you meant well. I don't mean to sound ungrateful. I mean, what you did with the backyard...the makeover...it's beautiful. But I'm so mad at you right now I have half a mind to charge you with grand theft."

Tom's tan, clean-shaven face lost the remainder of its usually good-natured, boyish charm.

"So that's the thanks I get. Nice one, Val. You know, I put up with a lot from you, but tonight takes the cake. I tell you 'I love you,' and you return the favor by telling me you're going to have me arrested. Not an even swap."

A pang of remorse hurtled toward my heart. I knocked it away with a baseball bat.

"Well, neither was you're swapping my mother's RV for a blasted tiki hut!"

Tom pulled a business card from his wallet and tossed it on the kitchen counter. "I guess it's true what they say. No good deed goes unpunished."

Tom glared at me, pursed his lips, shook his head and marched out the front door. He slammed it behind him. I waited until I heard the engine start and his SUV drive away before I picked up the card. Maybe I should have felt guilty. After all, Tom had meant well. But not a single speck of slithering guilt dared crawl close enough to be scalded by my boiling anger. Not *this* time. I was tired of always paying the tab for others good-intentioned misdeeds.

Why did everything nice have to come with a crap-smeared string attached?

I looked down at the business card. It read, "Lefty's Hauling: We make your troubles disappear!" The bitter irony forced a puff of jaded air through my pinched lips. It was 11 p.m. on a Saturday night. I took a chance and called the number. No one answered. The card stated the business was closed on Sundays. It seemed I was going to have to wait. Something I was definitely no good at.

Chapter Two

I idled away Sunday morning swinging in my new hammock, going back and forth as to whether I should call Tom and apologize or call Tom and rip him a new one. I should have been ecstatic. Tom had just told me he loved me for the very first time. I'd been contemplating whether to say it back to him when I'd been blindsided by the news he'd gone and traded away my mother for a thatch-roofed shack. How could the man have been so insensitive?

I scowled and looked across the freshly landscaped backyard. It was so gorgeous I nearly forgave Tom again. The comfy, macramé hammock I was swaying in was tied between two palm trees and offered a beautiful view of the sparkling Intracoastal Waterway. A set of six floral-cushioned lawn chairs formed a ring around a circular fire pit made of terracotta-hued pavers. Even the traitorous tiki hut was charming, with its shaggy, conical roof of thatched palm leaves. It was all so beautiful—and in need of a lifetime of constant maintenance.

By 9 a.m., the newly installed plants had already begun to wither in the tropical heat of the first day of May. I got out my old garden hose and spent the second half of the morning watering the freshly planted lantana bushes, canna lilies, pygmy date palms and St. Augustine grass. To save work, I took a quick trip to the little Ace Hardware store on Boca Ciega and bought a sprinkler to irrigate the neat swath of newly lain lawn.

When I returned, an itchy irritability crawled across my brain. Sweat dripped off my chin as I stood in the glaring sun and fiddled with the new sprinkler. I tried to set it to the correct angle. I clicked it to 45 degrees and turned on the tap. Before I could say, "Oh crap," the hose swelled up like a pregnant snake and blew the sprinkler off the end like a bottle rocket. It slammed into my shin, prompting me to scream all the curse words in my repertoire and perform the one-legged hip-hop. While I was dancing around, the hose, like a heckler in the audience, curled itself upward and, with deadly accuracy, shot a stream of cold water into my obscenity-hurling face. Given the horrid heat, it should have cooled me off. But the only thing the cold blast managed to refresh was my seething anger at Tom.

This dang landscaping is the gift that keeps on giving. Giving me more chores and responsibilities and ways to sweat my freaking butt off! Thanks a lot, Tom!

Soaked to my skin, I gave up and lay down in the hammock. I was drying off my clothes and cooling off my temper when that freaking jerk Guilty Conscience showed up and tried to convince me that maybe *I* had been the insensitive one.

Had I been wrong to grouse about Tom's beautiful and probably darn-expensive birthday gift? I gave my unwanted visitor an angry glare and a couple of Tanqueray and tonics. The second TNT, along with a Southern dollop of self-righteousness, had just begun to loosen guilt's whiny stranglehold on me when I heard a familiar voice call my name.

"Val?"

So much for enjoying the tranquility of my new backyard. Geez! Maybe I really was being an ungrateful sourpuss....

I took a tentative peek out of the hammock at the nosey, long-legged, horse-faced old woman in a gold bikini.

"Hi, Laverne."

Want to keep on reading? Awesome! Grab your copy now with the link below:

https://www.amazon.com/dp/B074W8VBFN

About the Author

Like the characters in my novels, I haven't lead a life of wealth or luxury. In fact, as it stands now, I'm set to inherit a half-eaten jar of Cheez Whiz...if my siblings don't beat me to it.

During my illustrious career, I've been a roller-skating waitress, an actuarial assistant, an advertising copywriter, a real estate agent, a house flipper, an organic farmer, and a traveling vagabond/truth seeker. But no matter where I've gone or what I've done, I've always felt like a weirdo.

I've learned a heck of a lot in my life. But getting to know myself has been my greatest journey. Today, I know I'm smart. I'm direct. I'm jaded. I'm hopeful. I'm funny. I'm fierce. I'm a pushover. And I have a laugh that makes strangers come up and want to join in the fun. In other words, I'm a jumble of opposing talents and flaws and emotions. And it's all good.

In some ways, I'm a lot like Val Fremden. My books featuring Val are not autobiographical, but what comes out of her mouth was first formed in my mind, and sometimes the parallels are undeniable. I drink TNTs. I had a car like Shabby Maggie. And I've started my life over four times, driving away with whatever earthly possessions fit in my car. And, perhaps most importantly, I've learned that friends come from unexpected places.